Amanda Minnie Douglas

Kathie's Aunt Ruth

Amanda Minnie Douglas

Kathie's Aunt Ruth

ISBN/EAN: 9783337366704

Printed in Europe, USA, Canada, Australia, Japan

Cover: Foto ©Andreas Hilbeck / pixelio.de

More available books at **www.hansebooks.com**

BY

AMANDA M. DOUGLAS,

AUTHOR OF "KATHIE'S THREE WISHES," "KATHIE'S SUMMER AT CEDARWOOD,"
"KATHIE'S SOLDIERS," "IN THE RANKS," "KATHIE'S HARVEST DAYS,"
"IN TRUST," ETC.

BOSTON:
LEE AND SHEPARD, PUBLISHERS.
1883.

UNIVERSITY PRESS: JOHN WILSON & SON,
CAMBRIDGE.

AGNES CLAIRE WORRALL.

—◆—

" Be good, sweet maid, and let who will be clever,
    Do noble things, not dream them, all day long;
So making life, death, and that vast forever,
    One grand, sweet song."

Woodside, 1870.

Kathie Stories.

---

1. KATHIE'S THREE WISHES.

2. KATHIE'S AUNT RUTH.

3. KATHIE'S SUMMER AT CEDARWOOD.

4. KATHIE'S SOLDIERS.

5. IN THE RANKS.

6. KATHIE'S HARVEST DAYS.

CONTENTS.

CHAPTER I.

PAGE

GETTING INTO TROUBLE 9

CHAPTER II.

ROB'S WEEK OF FUN 27

CHAPTER III.

WHAT STRAYED INTO THE POUND 54

CHAPTER IV.

KATHIE'S HOUSEKEEPING 66

CHAPTER V.

GOING TO A PARTY 81

CHAPTER VI.

GETTING OUT OF DEBT 101

CHAPTER VII.

JUST IN LUCK 121

CONTENTS.

CHAPTER VIII.

PLAYING NURSE 139

CHAPTER IX.

A GOOD SOLDIER 150

CHAPTER X.

A FRESH TRIAL 170

CHAPTER XI.

KATHIE'S CHRISTMAS 187

CHAPTER XII.

CRUMBS OF COMFORT 206

CHAPTER XIII.

TAKING UP THE CROSS 219

CHAPTER XIV.

OUT OF THE SHADOW AND IN THE SUN . . . 238

KATHIE'S AUNT RUTH.

CHAPTER I.

GETTING INTO TROUBLE.

"AUNT RUTH, will you drive out in the pony-carriage?" asked Kathie one morning. "Uncle Robert thinks that I can manage the horses very well."

Kathie looked so bright and winsome as she said this that Aunt Ruth smiled. "I think I must accept your invitation; the day is so very lovely that it will be a pleasure."

Kathie was delighted. Since Uncle Robert had given the children the ponies, Rob had taken out his mother and Aunt Ruth quite often. He seemed, boy-like, to have a natural aptitude for driving, while Kathie was rather timid. Mr. Meredith and her uncle had given her daily instructions, however, and she had now become quite a skilful little horse-woman.

She went to give her orders to Mr. Morrison, and by the time Aunt Ruth was ready the ponies pranced up the winding drive. The arrangement of the avenue shut off the barn and stable from the view of the house, bordered as it was with tall cedars, and added a picturesque air.

It was a very fine August morning. There had been a shower during the night, and the air was cool and fragrant. Everything looked fresh and green, and the dahlias, that had hung their heads in dusty languor, stood proudly erect in renewed brilliance. Birds carolled as gayly as in springtime.

Hugh Morrison helped Aunt Ruth in the carriage, and Kathie drove away with a smile of satisfaction. For a mile or so the ponies required her attention; but as they steadied down the child's face seemed to grow correspondingly grave.

"Of what are you thinking, Kathie?" Aunt Ruth asked, presently.

"O," and she looked up gayly, "I was thinking of the time Miss Jessie took us out in the sleigh, and how pleasant it was. Such a surprise too!"

"It was very kind, indeed, — one of the happy memories of our past life."

Kathie drew a long breath. "Something else came into my mind, Aunt Ruth. I feel as if I ought to return some of these favors to others."

"What particular person is to have this pleasure?" and Aunt Ruth smiled kindly.

A dainty little flush went up to her temples. "You know that Mrs. Gardiner has been very sick. She is getting better; and when I was there yesterday the doctor said that if she could go to ride it would do her a great deal of good. But there does not seem to be any one to take her; and then I thought how happy Miss Jessie made us last winter, and I would like to do the same thing, though she is not as poor as we were then. And she was very kind to us too. The day Uncle Robert came home, she told me that as soon as the strawberries were ripe mamma must send me to get some."

"It would be right pleasant, Kathie, as we know by experience. I am glad to find you so considerate."

"Then, Aunt Ruth, let us drive that way. If she knows that you trust me she may not feel at all afraid; and the ponies are so very gentle."

"I think that a good plan," answered Aunt Ruth. approvingly.

So on their return they went round by Mrs. Gardiner's. They passed the old house in their way.

"How odd it seems!" said Kathie. "I sometimes wonder if I really am the little girl who used to live there, and if all these wonderful things have happened to me since last Christmas!"

Lucy Gardiner had been sweeping the piazza and the broad-stones down the path. She stopped, broom in hand, delighted to see Kathie.

"Mamma is better!" she exclaimed, joyfully. "She walked out in the garden this morning. Will you come in?"

Kathie sprang down and tied the ponies, for Aunt Ruth preferred sitting still; it was so much exertion to get her out and in again.

"You can drive all by yourself, — is n't that splendid!" exclaimed Lucy, in wide-eyed astonish- 'ment. "And to have a pony!"

"I 'm coming in," said Kathie, with her cheery smile. "I want to see your mother a moment."

Mrs. Gardiner was in the sitting-room, pillowed in the rocking-chair. She held out her hand to Kathie with a pleased look.

"I saw you in the carriage," she said. "How much comfort you and Aunt Ruth must take together! And you are very kind to come so often."

"I wanted to — ask a favor this morning," Kathie began, timidly. "The doctor said you might go to ride, and I thought that I would like to take you if —"

"My dear Kathie," said Mrs. Gardiner, in surprise, "how thoughtful you are! Do you really mean to spend your time upon a poor sick woman when you might be enjoying it better?"

"But I seem to have so much time to play and all that, and no work to do, so I think I ought to be useful in some way. And it will be a pleasure. You see I brought Aunt Ruth, that you might know it was perfectly safe."

"I used to drive a good deal when I was a girl. We lived on a farm and had horses. I should not be at all afraid."

"And if you would go this afternoon —"

"Why, I think I might," she said, slowly, glancing out at the quivering sunshine and the low, easy carriage. "It would be a great treat, for I get so tired of staying here day after day, and they are so hurried at the shop that Mr. Gardiner cannot get off an hour."

Just then Lucy ran in, her dimpled face rosy with the exercise of work.

"Kathie has asked me to go out in her pretty carriage," said her mother.

"O mamma, is n't that delightful! I only wish some one would give me a pony."

Both of the girls looked at each other and then laughed. "I was thinking of the day your uncle asked you to direct him," said Lucy, and Kathie rejoined, "So was I."

"How grand you 'll be, mamma! I saw Kathie taking out Miss Jessie Darrell one day last week."

"Then if you will go this afternoon; will three be too early?"

"O no. I shall take a nap after dinner and be in a state to enjoy the drive wonderfully."

Lucy had to kiss Kathie half a dozen times before she let her go, and call her the dearest little thing in the world, and not a bit proud because she lived in a handsome house and had a pony.

So Kathie went away much pleased with her success, and drove directly home. The house was very quiet. Uncle Robert had gone to the next town and taken Freddy with him, while Rob and Dick Grayson were away on a small fishing expedition.

Aunt Ruth's room was considered a general sitting-room, and thither Kathie brought her work-basket, to rest herself, she said. Mrs. Alston was making her a dress, and she employed her leisure time working a pair of slippers for Uncle Robert. As they were to be a surprise, she had to do them when he was not present. Aunt Ruth read aloud to them.

They passed very many happy days together. Some of the village people thought Mrs. Alston exceedingly plain and deficient in both taste and ambition. But it was her desire, while the children were small at least, to live as simply as possible. Their one servant found herself not overworked, for the mistress took the charge of household matters, and Hugh, being very handy and obliging, did many little favors for them. It was Mrs. Alston's desire to make her brother's home as pleasant as she could, and not to burden him with unnecessary cares or expense.

A little before three Kathie set out again on her errand of kindness. Mrs. Gardiner was looking bright and expectant, and good-natured Irish Maggie, who was as strong in the arms as a man, helped her in the carriage. Lucy and Annie gave them three cheers.

The day was still beautiful, and the air fragrant with the resinous odor of the pines and cedars. Mrs. Gardiner drew long, reviving breaths, and felt that she could hardly thank Kathie sufficiently for the pleasure. They drove slowly through the shady roads, Kathie talking in her simple fashion, which was extremely entertaining. She enjoyed Mrs. Gardiner's delight as fully as if it had been her very own.

"It is such a luxury to get out," the lady said. "For six weeks I have been confined to the house. I never was sick so long before, and it has been very tiresome. Annie and Lucy have been so good, though, that it has lightened my anxiety. Kathie, you hardly know how happy pleasant, helpful children make their mothers."

Kathie was a very humble little girl, and she thought now of the many times she might have been useful to her mother when she had gone to play instead. But latterly she *had* tried.

When they returned, for Mrs. Gardiner was not strong enough for a very long drive, the two little girls sat on the piazza in their clean gingham dresses and white aprons.

"O Mrs. Gardiner, can't they go a little while?" asked Kathie, with great earnestness.

"I am afraid we shall trespass on your kindness, my dear child."

"O no. It will be such fun for us all."

"And you think your mother would n't disapprove?" was Mrs. Gardiner's doubtful question.

"I am very sure."

Lucy and Annie were overjoyed. They were as gay as little larks, quite as noisy too when they were out of hearing. They passed several of the school-girls, and Lottie Thorne and her mother trudging along on foot. Lottie gave them a disdainful nod.

"You don't care, — do you?" said Annie. "But Lottie is going to the sea-shore, and she has ever so many pretty new dresses."

"I 'd a good deal rather have a pony," said Lucy. "This is just splendid."

Kathie thought so too as the ponies trotted along.

2

As for sea-side, there was beautiful Silver Lake,
and their pretty house was nicer than any hotel.

So they laughed and talked, and enjoyed themselves to the utmost.   Once or twice when Kathie
would have turned they begged her to go just a
little bit farther, and when they reached home they
were surprised to find it so late.   Mrs. Gardiner was
lying down, but she declared herself much refreshed.
" Indeed, I feel as if I should get up to-morrow and
go to work," she said, laughingly.

Then Kathie went home quite well satisfied with
her afternoon.   How delightful it was to make
people happy !

" You 're a pretty one," said Rob, in no very pleasant tone, as she was walking the ponies leisurely up
the avenue.   " Here you 've had the horses the whole
day !   I promised Dick Grayson that he might try
them, and he waited and waited.   It 's real mean of
you ; they 're as much mine as yours ! "

" I did not know you were coming back, Rob, and
then it was n't altogether for my own pleasure — "

" I don't know what you call your own pleasure !
You and the Gardiner girls have been cutting around
all the afternoon, and it is n't a bit fair."

Aunt Ruth had told Rob that Kathie had gone to take out Mrs. Gardiner, but he was too much vexed to admit this fact, especially as rambling down the street with Dick Grayson he had caught sight of the three girls having a good time.

"What is n't fair?" asked Uncle Robert, coming forward. "Why, Kathie, we thought you lost."

"She had the horses all the morning, and this afternoon, when I wanted them half an hour or so, she was off with the Gardiner girls. You know you said that we were to take turns."

"And you think Kathie has had more than her 'turn,' do you? Kathie, you should not be the first to transgress."

"I am very sorry that I disappointed Rob," Kathie said, soberly. "I did not suppose he would be home until night."

Coming as it did in the midst of her enjoyment, Kathie felt her face flush and a lump swelled in her throat, so she walked quietly to the house. She bathed her face and hands and changed her dress, then went to Aunt Ruth's room.

"Well, my dear," exclaimed Aunt Ruth; but she stopped at sight of the grave face. "Did n't you have a pleasant time?"

"Yes, it was very nice, but — Rob wanted the horses."

"And I told him where you had gone."

"Did you?" said Kathie, relieved. "But afterwards I took Annie and Lucy. They were so delighted, Aunt Ruth, that I kept going farther and farther. I suppose it was wrong."

"No, I cannot see that it was. Rob expected to be gone all day, and you certainly were at liberty to make any arrangements you chose. We'll leave it to Uncle Robert."

He was crossing the hall at that moment and entered. "What weighty matter is to be left to me?" he asked.

Aunt Ruth began to tell the story with their talk of the morning. Uncle Robert drew Kathie to a seat on his knee and threaded her soft curls with his fingers. He had felt quite like blaming her a few moments ago, for he could not endure the thought of her growing selfish, but Aunt Ruth's version put the matter in a different light.

"My dear child, why did n't you stop to explain?" he said, softly. "If Rob had known, he would not have been so quick to blame."

"He did know," said Aunt Ruth. "Up to this time he has driven the horses much more than Kathie, and he begins to feel that he has the best right. I think it is just as necessary that Kathie should give her friends pleasure as that Rob should minister to his."

"Aunt Ruth is right"; and Uncle Robert kissed the flushed cheek. "But my little girl need never be afraid to tell me anything, whether she is in the right or wrong."

Kathie twined her arms tenderly about his neck, very glad indeed to find that he did not consider that she had committed a grave fault, as she feared from his reproof out on the walk; and then she gave him the history of her afternoon.

"Under the circumstances I do not think you were at fault. Rob was not expected home so early, and he had left no particular word that all should be in readiness for his convenience. You know the bargain?" and her uncle smiled.

"But Rob has n't broken it!" she said, quickly.

"He has not been quite kind or generous."

Freddy rushed in to show a wonderful top that Uncle Robert had bought him. As it spun round it had exactly the appearance of a butterfly with its wings spread, and being painted in bright colors the illusion was perfectly sustained. Leaving him to entertain Kathie, Uncle Robert went in pursuit of his namesake.

Rob was not in an angelic mood by any means. First, the fishing expedition had not been a brilliant success. They had rambled up and down the river-bank, eaten their luncheon in the shade, and taken a drowsy rest; but the fish would n't bite. Then he had coaxed Dick home with him under promise of trying the ponies, and he felt rather ill-used to have them gone. Upon complaining to Aunt Ruth he had learned the facts, but when he came upon Kathie and her friends the laughing faces exasperated him still more. It almost seemed as if Kathie had used Mrs. Gardiner for an excuse, though he knew down in his heart that his little sister would scorn a falsehood. He was rather pleased that Uncle Robert did not acquit her without a word. Then he had followed Hugh to the stable and tormented Prince until he whined in pain, and now he was switching off some rank red clover-blossoms.

His uncle met him with a frank smile, and yet

there was a steady look in the pleasant eyes not easy to evade.

"Rob," he said, "do you think you were quite just or gentlemanly to Kathie a little while ago?"

Rob hung his head and switched away more vigorously than before.

His uncle caught the little slender rod gently in his hand and said, gravely, "I want you to listen to me."

"Kathie had them all day," he ejaculated, rather sullenly.

"But you knew her errand this afternoon?"

"She was off with the Gardiner girls when I saw her. I think she might have come home earlier. I only wanted the ponies for a little while."

"And she did not imagine that you would be home or care to drive. You know one was to be generous as well as the other."

"Well, I have n't had a chance to be ungenerous to-day," said Rob, grimly. "Kathie 's had it all her own way."

"And what did you say to her?"

"It was enough to vex a fellow," was his lame justification.

"Whose patience and consideration are not wonderfully extensive. I am very sorry that you spoke so harshly and accused her unjustly, since you knew the reason, — that she had gone to give a sick friend a little change and pleasure."

Rob kicked the gravel in the path rather spitefully. "If she had not stayed with the girls," he said.

"What would you have done had it been boys instead?"

Rob could not venture upon an answer. To say that he should have come directly home would have been stretching probability beyond its verge. He felt that he was in the wrong, and kept silence.

"So I think you owe Kathie an apology."

Uncle Robert's sway had been gentle but firm. He rarely insisted that his nephew should do any particular thing, but he brought a very strong moral pressure that it was quite difficult to evade. The boy was rather cross and sulky than humble. In fact Rob had allowed himself to get altogether out of gear, and felt worse than ever when he found that he could lay the blame on no one, except Robert Alston, who was in his mind a rather unfortunate and suffering individual.

"I leave you to make it up with Kathie," Uncle Robert said, cheerily, turning away.

Girls were unmitigated nuisances. If the world had only been peopled with boys instead, and if they could only do anything without being brought to a strict account! Rob sighed in a heart-breaking fashion and went down to the lake. If he only had a boat!

He came home just in time for supper. His mother was passing through the hall with a dish of fruit in her hand.

"How tired you look!" she said, in her soft, motherly voice, different from any other voice in the world. "You should not have gone out after Dick Grayson went away." Then she passed her cool hand over his forehead.

Rob winked away something wonderfully like a tear. It was the "foes within" rather than any physical exertion.

Uncle Robert had said the best way to repair a wrong was to acknowledge it immediately. And after all Rob's bravado out in the woods he felt that he had been at fault. Giants reared their heads in palaces as well as the little brown house over yonder, and it was just as necessary to fight them here as it had been there.

So he washed his face in good cold water that cleared the cobwebs from his brain ; he combed the tangles out of his curly hair and felt quite like another boy.

Running down stairs, he met Kathie looking fresh and sweet as a rose.

" I was as rude as a bear to you a little while ago," he said, in a hurried whisper.   " And I — "

" Never mind.   I was having such a nice time that I quite forgot about every one else ; but you may have the ponies all day to-morrow, — that will make it about straight again."

He was n't a bit afraid to meet Uncle Robert's eye, and he felt as light and cheery about the heart as you please.   He even went and had a nice time with Prince, who wagged his shaggy tail and looked out of his great delighted eyes as only a dog can look.   And that evening he and Uncle Robert had a good long talk about the old Australian life.

CHAPTER II.

ROB'S WEEK OF FUN.

Rob's vacation was signalized by the promised visit to New York, and he enjoyed it immensely. It made no difference to him that all the fashionable people had gone to Saratoga or Newport. They had left the Park, the hotels, the broad bay, and the islands, and Rob felt that when the week came to an end he had not seen half, though he had gone about continually. He pitied Kathie a good deal for having been a girl and not able to enjoy the sights in his fashion.

"But I had a lovely time," she said, contentedly.

"And she brought me home a locomotive," put in Fred, as a sort of settler for the superiority of her visit.

"But she had a wonderful purse, and I have not," he returned.

Truth to tell, he had not thought about bringing them anything. Rob was always too well satisfied

with his own enjoyment to consider the wants or
pleasures of others.   He was not more selfish than
a great many boys, it is true, but he claimed a
pretty large right to think first of himself.   And
then it seemed to him that they had about everything they wanted.

"We must begin to plan a little for the future,"
said Uncle Robert, as they were spending the evening in Aunt Ruth's room.   "It will soon be the
first of September, and Rob's vacation will come to
an end."

"O dear!" and the boy sighed.

"Why, Rob!" exclaimed his mother, in amaze-
ment, "have n't you had enough play in the last
six weeks?   I believe you have not been still a
moment, except when you were asleep."

"But a whole year again seems so long.   I wish
I was a grown-up man, like Uncle Robert, and did
n't have anything to do."

"Well, what would be the first step?"

"I 'd buy a yacht and sail all around the world,
going from one port to another, and have lots of
adventures.   I 'd learn all about different countries,
and I 'd rescue people from shipwreck, and O, ever
so many things!"

"I'm afraid I can't make a public benefactor out of you, Rob, nor a man of pleasure, so you will have to moderate your desires."

"But I might go to Australia and make a fortune."

"Rob, for the one who succeeds there are ten failures. And at present it is boyhood, not manhood, for which we have to plan. A good education, good moral habits, and strength of character, form the best capital that one can have; and now you must be acquiring it. You will be fifteen in the winter."

"I think I should like to go to boarding-school," Rob announced, after a pause.

"I don't know that I am quite prepared to part with you upon so short an acquaintance," said his uncle, laughingly. "I was talking to Mr. Grayson about the Academy, and I find that he is very well satisfied with it."

"O," exclaimed Mrs. Alston, "I don't want Rob to go away from home at present. And now the idea of his growing to manhood is not attractive. My little Rob!" and his mother placed her hand affectionately on his shoulder.

"But I'm not to be a baby always," he said, with a good deal of big-boy dignity.

"I used to think," said Kathie, "that our good fortune would begin when Rob was a man and could work for us."

Rob felt in his heart that he was very well satisfied to have the good fortune now.

"So I think it will be best for Rob to try the Academy for a year at least."

"The boys are snobby," declared Rob, "all but Dick Grayson, and old Crittenden's awful strict; they don't have but precious little fun."

"The fun had better be out of school, my boy," returned his uncle, gravely. "Fred must keep on where he is, I suppose, for they have no pupils younger than ten at the Academy."

Rob was rather delighted with this, though he did not say so; but Freddy was as bad as the Old Man of the Mountains to him.

"And what am I to do?" asked Kathie.

"We are coming to that. Aunt Ruth thinks she may want you presently. Dr. Markham desires her to come to New York about the middle of next month, and it will be best for your mamma to go with her."

Kathie slipped her hand within Aunt Ruth's.

Part of Uncle Robert's errand to the city had been to make arrangements for Aunt Ruth's removal; and though she was very much interested in having the invalid restored to health, her tender little heart shrank from the pain and suffering that must be endured.

"And while we are all away, you will have to be housekeeper, Kathie," her uncle said, cheerily. "I want to see how well you can all get along."

"But am I not to go to school at all?" asked Kathie, wonderingly.

"I will give you a few lessons, and you must study some by yourself. There will be a good deal of excitement and anxiety, and as you are my little right-hand man, I don't want you to have too much on your mind."

"Well I 'm bound to have one good week of fun!" said Rob, as he went off to his room.

That was Monday night. Early Tuesday morning, before he was out of bed, he began planning what he should do. Harry Cox had asked him to come over to his house. His cousin from New York was there, and had brought his gun, and it pleased the two boys very much to be allowed to use it.

Rob had teased a little for a gun. His mother, having a great dread of fire-arms, persuaded his uncle not to indulge him at present, so he had grumbled in secret about women always being afraid. Harry had said, "Come one day this week, before school commences, and we 'll have lots of fun." So Rob thought he could not do a better thing than to accept the invitation at once.

"But you were at Harry's on Friday," his mother said.

"I promised to come again; his cousin Jim is staying there."

"Come home quite early then."

Harry and Jim were just starting off to the woods with gun, game-bag, and dog. They were glad to see Rob, and the party trudged along to the woods, where there were plenty of squirrels. Jim Fields quite prided himself upon being a good shot; but he was nearly seventeen.

The gun being his, he tried his luck first; and the boys thought it splendid. What opinion the poor little birds and squirrels had was quite another matter. Harry used to be tender-hearted at first, but boys soon get over these feelings, I am sorry to say. He had practised considerably, and now waited impatiently for his turn to come.

"There," said Jim, "beat that if you can; now I 'll rest a little while."

With that he stretched himself upon the grass and began reading a dime-novel, giving the boys a watchful glance now and then.

"I know I could pop over some of them just as handy as you please if I could only get a chance at them," exclaimed Harry; "come a little farther down."

They rambled slowly about, talking in low tones, and presently they espied a fine fellow sitting almost in the crotch of a tree, looking as if he had hidden away there. Harry took aim and, sure enough, down he fell.

"There," he announced, much elated, "I told you so; and there goes a bird! Just wait till I have another shot."

"That was n't the bargain," said Rob.

"Boys," shouted a voice from a distance, "what luck? Whose shot this time?"

"Just see what a hit, Jim, — straight through the head!" and Harry held up the shattered squirrel; "I 'd like to go down by the creek."

3

"Well, be careful; and you too, Rob Alston."

So Jim found another soft spot in the mossy woods and resigned himself to his book.

Rob insisted upon having his turn next. He shot into a flock of birds, scattering them in every direction, but not even touching a feather.

" What an aim !" laughed Harry, scornfully. "Now you just watch me."

Considering that Rob was a year the oldest, this command was rather mortifying; and when Harry took his turn three or four times in succession, Rob's patience began to fail. At first he was a trifle sulky; but he could not quietly endure seeing another have all the fun.

During a little lull in Harry's ardor a red squirrel crept out cautiously and ran along the fence.

" Now !" said Rob, in a whisper; "just this once. See there !"

"No, I 'll be sure to bring him. You could n't."

Both had hold of the gun. Rob thought Harry real mean and gave a jerk, and somehow Harry's hand slipped. It all happened in a second, and Rob was keeping one eye on the squirrel, but the gun went off and Harry, uttering a loud cry, fell to the ground.

Rob screamed too. He was so frightened at first that he trembled like a leaf, then he ran off, for he could n't bear to look at Harry. He came clear up to the spot where Jim was reading before the latter stirred.

"Oh!" he exclaimed, breathless and pale as a ghost, — "O, come quick; I 've killed Harry!"

He was too much frightened to make any excuse, for it seemed to him by this time that Harry must surely be dead.

Jim made a bound, then turned to ask "Where?" and the two ran on together.

Harry was not killed, but sitting up against a tree, groaning vigorously, yet some blood was trickling through the leg of his brown linen trousers. He looked pretty pale, however.

"What is it? How did it happen? Where are you hurt, Harry?" asked Jim, in a breath.

"Rob jerked the gun and it went off! I think my leg 's broken to splinters," the sufferer whined.

Jim had his wits about him and ripped up the pantaloons. Rob grew rather white about the mouth, expecting to see a ghastly wound. Jim wiped the blood away with a handful of soft moss, and there were two or three scratches. The revulsion was so great that Rob had hard work to keep from laughing.

"O dear!" groaned Harry.

"Why, it's nothing, fortunately for you. There may be a stray shot lodged under the skin, but it will not do much damage. Rob Alston, did n't you know any better than to jerk the gun away from him? Why, you might have killed him!"

"I did n't mean to hurt him, and it was my turn. He 'd been shooting all the time."

"Well, the gun belongs to *my* cousin," said Harry, ungraciously. Generally I will admit that Harry was a very good-tempered boy; but he was wont to become very much excited over hunting expeditions, and now he was smarting with the pain of his wound.

Rob might have confessed that he was sorry a moment before, but now he was angry. He bit his lip hard, that he might not say anything.

"Rob," said Jim, in a grave tone, "you must never do the like again under any circumstances, or something might happen to make you miserable for your whole life. And you know you promised to agree about taking turns."

"Harry would n't," Rob flung out, indignantly, ready to cry from excitement and the peculiar revulsion of feeling that had followed Jim's announcement.

In the mean while Jim was bandaging Harry's leg with his handkerchief. "Now," he said, " we will stop at the druggist's and see if it is mortal."

"I don't believe I can walk," was the faint response.

"O yes, you can; Rob will help you on one side. It 's better to have it properly cared for. Come!"

They lifted him up, and when once started went on quite bravely. Harry was not much of a soldier; but the young doctor who made his head-quarters at the drug-store laughed at him a little, extracted two or three shot, and bade him not to run a race for the next day or two. Then he said, " If you 'll get in my wagon I 'll take you home."

"Good by!" exclaimed Rob, turning away.

"Don't worry yourself about it," said Jim; "Harry will soon be running around again. Only in future be more careful with fire-arms."

It was about noon, and Rob could hardly decide what to do. If he went home now he must tell the

story and worry his mother, who would be sure to
think of all that might have. happened; so he rambled off down to the river, and took a swim in
the shade of the overhanging trees; but it seemed
dull music. His fun was spoiled that day; besides,
he was growing very hungry. He went up to the
village, and stopped at the baker's to buy some cake
with a few pennies that he had. Then he sauntered
around until, utterly tired out, he turned his steps
homeward. His mother was tying up a vine on the
kitchen porch.

"Why, how early you are!" she said. "Did you
have a nice time?" and then she fancied that he did
not look very happy.

If it had not been for alarming her, he certainly
would have told the truth, he thought. Indeed, he
had a guilty feeling about it, and resolved to confess
to Uncle Rob at once.

"Pretty nice," he said, faintly.

"Charlie Darrell and Miss Jessie are here."

"O, are they?" then Rob passed through the hall,
and went up to his room to make himself presentable.

"O Rob," began Freddy, who was rummaging
round, "won't you make me a rabbit-house? Charlie

Darrell says that he will give me two teeny little white rabbits."

" Yes, to-morrow," answered Rob, hurrying into some clean clothes.

Then he hastened down to the lawn, where they were all sitting in the shade.

" I am so glad you have come," said Kathie ; " we were wishing for you to play a little croquet. I don't believe I shall ever learn."

" But there are not enough of us ! "

" Miss Jessie said that we could try it."

Rob felt that he ought to be particularly obliging, so he went for the box of balls and mallets.

There was a good deal of amusement, if not much science. In the height of their laughing at Kathie's blunders, Uncle Robert made his appearance. Then they coaxed mamma out, and had quite a game. Presently Hannah announced supper.

They spent a very pleasant hour together afterward ; but when Miss Jessie and Charlie had gone home one of the workmen came to discuss some plans with Uncle Robert, and so Rob went off to bed without having told his story. After all, he guessed that it did n't make much matter. Harry would be

well in a few days, the doctor said, and he would
speak of it the first time that he had a chance.
After all, it was not very much his fault ; and his
conscience did not trouble him enough to keep
him awake.

"Rob!" shouted Freddy in his ear the next morning. "Come, get up! You promised to make my
rabbit-house, you know !"

"Well, you need n't rouse me in the middle of
the night," exclaimed Rob, sleepily.

Freddy presented a rather comical picture as he
stood tugging away at the leg of his trousers.

"'T is n't the middle of the night," he said,
sturdily. "It 's broad morning !"

"Well," returned Rob, "there will be no peace, I
suppose, so I may as well get about it."

He wondered a little how Harry felt and if he
meant to be angry with him. Would n't it be right
to go over and inquire about him ?

After breakfast he went to work in good earnest.
Freddy was delighted, and made himself so helpful
that he was a great bother, but Rob kept his patience
remarkably well. Mr. Morrison marked out some
stuff for him, and Rob· sawed and hammered like a

Trojan.   There was to be a little covered house and a yard enclosed with palings, as Mrs. Alston said they would do too much injury to the trees and shrubs if they ran about.

Uncle Robert came to oversee a little, and praised his nephew's skill. By noon the place was pretty well finished. An hour or so afterward Dick Grayson came over, and the two boys soon painted it. A very pretty looking place it was.

"Now," said Rob, "if Kathie does n't want the horses we 'll have a nice drive. Freddy, you must keep away from this paint; now remember."

Rob picked up his tools and ran away up stairs. Hearing Kathie singing, he tumbled them on the bench and went to ask her. No, she did not care to go out, but if he went, Aunt Ruth wanted him to do an errand. So he started to learn what it was, and then went to order the horses. He had to take a last view of the building and command Freddy for the fiftieth time to keep away. He dressed himself in a hurry at the last, and as he was going down stairs remembered that he had not taken care of his tools nor locked the workroom. He could not run back and do it now, though, and he *guessed* that

Freddy would be kept busy admiring the rabbit-house.

They had a very pleasant drive, and Rob returned home in fine spirits. The first thing that met his eye as he entered Aunt Ruth's room was Freddy sitting quietly in an arm-chair, his hand bandaged and in a sling. Uncle Robert was reading to him.

" Why, what 's the matter ? " asked Rob.

" O, I sawed my hand off ! " and with that Fred began to cry.

" It does n't hurt much now," said his uncle, " and you know you were to be a brave boy."

" Freddy, you did n't go meddling with my tools, — did you ? " asked Rob, rather sharply.

Freddy whined and began to make excuses. " I was only trying to saw a little stick."

" And so he disobeyed orders and marched into forbidden territory, and you, Robert, were very care-less to leave your tools scattered around. I was quite surprised at the disorder."

" I was in a great hurry," said Rob, apologetically.

" Then you might have locked the door. I was very strongly inclined to do it and keep the key."

Rob felt that he should have gone back, and he

could not plead forgetfulness, so he was silent for a moment, then he asked soberly if Fred's hand was seriously hurt.

"Quite a severe flesh wound. I hope, Rob, that I shall not have to ask you to be careful for the next three months at least."

"I'm sure you won't," returned the boy, confidently.

Then his mother talked to him a little about being so careless, and Rob's temper was sadly ruffled. He thought he ought to have some credit for amusing Freddy all the morning, but no one ever seemed to appreciate the good things he did, and a great fuss was always made over the accidents.

Poor Rob did n't enjoy his evening very much, and was glad to go to bed. These two days had been failures.

The next morning he resolved that he would be extra good. His conscience still troubled him a little about Harry, and now it seemed so hard to tell.

He put his tools in order, made the room nice and tidy, then pulled some weeds out of his flower-bed and tied up his dahlias. Afterward he took his boat down to the lake to sail it, and Freddy wanted to go

with him.   At first he felt tempted to refuse, but on
second thoughts he acquiesced.

Rob, with his uncle's assistance, had made a very
pretty little ship, painted tastefully, and named " The
Jessie."   Freddy was always delighted to watch it
as it floated gracefully along the shore, its sails gently
filling with wind. He found a stick and was extremely
anxious to give it a little assistance, which Rob
forbade.   Then he picked up some dry leaves and set
them floating, beating the water to make waves and
foam.

"Don't!" said Rob a time or two, and then he
went farther down to escape the annoyance.

There was a tiny cove with a very shallow shore
edge half filled with large stones.   Fred had watched
Rob and Kathie jump from one to another, but he
had been forbidden to do it alone. He saw Rob going
slowly down, half hidden by the cedars, so he resolved
to venture.   He succeeded bravely and found it great
fun. If he could only get on the big rock and be
Robinson Crusoe! His feet were quite wet by the
exploit, but he was enjoying himself hugely, when
Rob called "Freddy!" Now if he could only
scamper back in time!

Alas! With his first bound he soused into the water. Rob heard the splash, but did not suppose it anything more than a stone. A scream followed it very soon, and he ran to see what was the matter. There was Fred floundering about, his nose, eyes, and ears full of water. As he was in no danger of drowning, Rob stopped to pull off his shoes and roll up his trousers.

"O you torment!" he exclaimed, giving him a jerk.

Fred's wounded hand had been hurt by the fall, and he was crying with pain and fright. Rob dragged him to the shore rather ungently.

"I have a good mind to send you home alone. You ought to have a whipping!"

"O, my hand! Don't run so fast, Rob! O dear! O dear!"

"Mother," exclaimed Rob, as they came in sight of the kitchen, "Fred 's been climbing over the stones and has fallen in the water. He 's the worst and most troublesome boy that I ever saw. He ought to have a whipping and be sent to bed."

"Why did you let him climb over the stones?" Mrs. Alston asked, in mild reproach.

"He went off to sail his boat," sobbed Fred. "He

never watched me at all, and I wanted to play Robinson Crusoe. I had a big stick for Friday. And if
he had n't hollered I would n't ha' tumbled into the
water. My hand hurts so — O dear!"

"Robert, I think you might take better care of
Freddy, and, Freddy, you will have to be punished
for disobeying. Come up stairs and get on some dry
clothes."

Rob thought of his boat and flung himself out of
the room. He ran down to the lake as fast as possible, but there was his boat half-way across. If he
only *had* stopped to take it out of the water! He
stamped his feet in anger and despair, and then he
gave way to some passionate tears. Everything
would go wrong. There never was such an unlucky
boy in the world. He was always blamed for other
people's faults, and if he had something particularly
nice, it was sure to meet with an accident. Dick
Grayson never had any trouble, nor Charlie Darrell;
but everything did happen to him!

Then he espied Uncle Robert in the road below,
and he ran down to him with a woe-begone face.

"Why, Rob, what now?" asked his uncle, in astonishment.

So Rob related his misadventure about the boat, and this had to take in Fred's graver complication.

"I guess it has n't been a very funny week," said his uncle, with a quiet smile that meant a good deal.

"Funny!"

"Yes. You set out to have a good deal of fun in this your last week, you know."

"And it 's all been trouble! How can we get the boat?"

"You see the wind is blowing it over to the opposite shore. I cannot think of any better way than to walk round."

He turned as if to go, and Rob was pleased with the idea of having company.

"Rob," he said presently, in a grave tone, "I want a little talk with you. I have just been to see Harry Cox."

Rob stood still in the path. He gave his uncle one glance, then his eyes drooped and his face was scarlet.

"I can't tell you how pained and hurt I felt when I heard of the accident this morning. And you have not even been to inquire about him."

Rob felt so thoroughly ashamed that he almost wished the ground would open and swallow him.

"Were you afraid to speak of it?"

"I did n't want to worry mamma," said Rob, hesitatingly. "She 's so afraid of fire-arms."

"That excuse would not apply to me."

There was a great struggle going on within Rob's heart and conscience. After his late mishaps he was sore and disposed to be resentful, and yet he had a dim suspicion that he was not altogether in the right.

"Rob, my dear boy," said his uncle, gravely, "I want you to believe that I love you and to have confidence in my regard. I have undertaken to fill the place of a father to you, but as I have not a father's authority I depend upon you to make the task easier for me by showing that you do trust me. I should like most of all to be your dearest friend, and have you feel free to come to me in doubt or trouble or difficulty of any kind. And when I fail I feel very, very sorry."

Something in the tone touched Rob deeply. There was in the depths of his heart a peculiar nobility, and such an appeal roused him when harsher means would have driven him to sulky silence.

"Uncle Robert," he said, huskily, turning and placing his hand on his uncle's shoulders, and looking at him with honest tears in his eyes, "I did mean to tell you, but so many things came in my way. I was so sorry about it too, but it *was* partly Harry's fault. And I 've been frightened and worried all the time. Is Harry very angry with me ?"

"Will you tell me frankly how it happened?" asked his uncle, not answering his question.

Rob thought a moment. He knew his uncle would not want to hear him justify himself. He was rather apt to shirk the truth and make weak excuses.

"I 'll try," he said, quite humbly for him. "Harry's cousin, Jim Fields, has a gun, and he taught us both to use it. Mr. Cox did n't object any, but— I — was afraid to ask on mamma's account. You know she said so much against my having a gun. They go hunting nearly every day, and I had been once before with them. Jim said Harry and I should take turns, and so we did the first time. Well, on Tuesday Harry would hardly let me try at all, but after he had fired a good many times, I spied a

4

squirrel and took the gun, when he said I could n't shoot it and that he would. So we both had hold of it, pulling, and it went off."

It was a great effort for Rob to tell the story as fairly as he did. His uncle knew this from the little breaks that came in his voice.

"Thank you, Rob," he said, " for being brave enough to tell just the truth. Harry told me the story this morning also, and very generously took all the blame."

" Then he is n't — " and Rob drew a long breath of relief, feeling very much as if he wanted to cry.

" He feels a good deal hurt that you have not been over to see him. And I can't tell you, Rob, how it pained me to think that he had more true courage than my boy."

" But he acted like a great baby when it happened."

" He admitted that he was very much frightened."

" Uncle Robert," the boy said, "I hate cowards and sneaks, and I don't mean to be one. I suppose it was because I had been doing something that mamma and you would not approve of that I had not the courage to tell. And yet I don't see what harm there is in a boy's having a gun."

"I do not think there is any particular harm in it, or in learning to shoot. It leads to one evil that I deprecate sincerely, — the practice of boys shooting at every little bird, which is wanton cruelty. If you are just exercising your skill, any mark will do as well. I should have bought you a gun if your mother had not objected so strongly. I resolved then that some time we would go on a little tour, camping out, and I would give you some instructions."

"O Uncle Robert!" he exclaimed, gratefully.

"I am trying to win your love, and to deserve it as well," was the rejoinder.

Rob clasped his arms around his uncle's neck. He was not a bit ashamed to cry then. "O, please do trust me again," he sobbed; "please help me to be good. I do. try sometimes, but it seems such hard work, and everything goes against me."

"I do not believe it is ever very easy. You have some grave faults that I should like to see you correct. You rarely think how anything will affect another person, and you are always so strongly intent upon your own pleasure or wishes. Men of this stamp are careless and apt to become hard and unscrupulous. I want to see you grow up into a noble and useful man, and you must lay the foundation in boyhood."

Rob felt very grave and tender at heart. " I believe I am selfish now," he said, presently.

" And I want you to cultivate that true moral courage that does not shrink from facing any difficulty that one may be betrayed into by a thoughtless act. You will learn by experience that all such secrets grow to be an immense burden, and you will feel very miserable in carrying them about. Now I wish you to go and see Harry. I am sorry that you have been so unfriendly."

" And what about mamma ? "

" Had you rather tell her, or have her learn it from some other person? It came to me quite by accident."

" I 'll tell her," Rob said, slowly and yet with earnestness.

By this time they had reached the opposite side of the lake, and the boat was drifting in. Uncle Robert cut a slender branch, with a crook at the end, and towed it to the shore. They walked quietly homeward, Rob revolving many things in his mind. He remembered that after he had been sick he had turned over a new leaf, and for a while events had gone smoothly; but with prosperity had come a good deal of carelessness.

"Mother," he said, finding her alone in the dining-room arranging the table, " I think it was partly my fault that Freddy fell in; I was n't watching him."

" Fred must learn to obey and do just as he is told. He is growing too thoughtless."

So Freddy had a dinner of bread and water up in his room, and no one was allowed to share his confinement.   Rob felt really sorry about it; but in the afternoon he went over to see Harry Cox, and the boys had a long, pleasant talk.   Harry possessed a genial, forgiving nature, and he had always been great friends with Rob.

There had not been very much fun in the week, he concluded.   Was it because he had thought of himself first, and all the time ?   It did look rather mean and selfish to care simply for one's own gratification and let others be pleased as best they might.

" I *will* try," he said softly to himself, after his evening prayer.

CHAPTER III.

WHAT STRAYED INTO THE POUND.

" I don't see what has become of all my gimlets,"
said Rob, after his first day's school. " I had three,
and they have all disappeared. I used the last one
the day I was making Fred's rabbit-house. You did
n't carry it away ? " to Freddy, who was entertaining
himself with a procession of animals from Noah's Ark.

" No, I 'm sure I did n't. And I can't find Noah
or the elephant. Kathie, have you had them ? "

They all laughed at this. Fred was rather non-
plussed. A quizzical look came in Uncle Robert's
eyes.

" Well, what have *you* lost, Kathie ? " he asked.

" O Fred ! you know Uncle Robert was going to
have a pound. I can't think whether anything of
mine has strayed into it or not," she said, with an
arch and amused expression.

" Three gimlets," declared Rob, with a mirthful
twist of his lip. " How much is the fine ? "

"I have been quietly confiscating articles for about a month, so you see that I did not begin immediately."

"O Uncle Robert, let us have an auction or a redemption," begged Kathie.

"Well, I think I will, only I do not know what fine to attach. I have such a store on hand that I should be glad to dispose of them."

Rob looked grave. Perhaps there were more than three gimlets in duress.

"Five cents for each article," exclaimed Kathie.

"Would n't that come rather hard on Fred?" asked Aunt Ruth.

"Well, then, a penny for Fred, and five cents for Rob and me."

"How about that, Rob?"

Rob looked rather dubious, it must be confessed. On the first of every week his uncle gave him some pocket-money, and he hated to lay out a great deal of it in the beginning for such a purpose, as now, when he came to think of it, he *had* missed a good many things during the past month.

"I am afraid it will break me," he said, laughingly.

"We will say a cent apiece. Do you hear that,

Freddy ?   Every one who has an article in my pound must pay a cent to redeem it."

"Aunt Ruthie's keeping my money."

"We'll bring on the elephant then"; and Uncle Robert left the room, returning with a covered basket. Inside were several packages wrapped in paper.

"I put them together once a week," said their uncle. "We will take the first week in August. A child's history found in the summer-house."

"Rob's !"

Rob reached out his hand. "We had better do the paying in a lump," he said.

"A gimlet picked up on the kitchen table, an odd glove found on the library table, three fish-hooks and a lead on the veranda, a partially made gutta-percha ring from the sideboard, two boat sails — "

"There, I never could imagine where they went," interrupted Rob. "I was sure I hunted high and low for them !"

Hannah gave them to me. They were left in the kitchen, or rather on the kitchen window-sill, and a whiff of wind blew them into the bread she was mixing."

There was a general laugh at this.

"We will say six articles, then, for the first week. Now, a partly finished sketch of the boat-house and lake."

"Mine," declared Kathie, with a smile. "Where did I leave it, I wonder?"

"In the library. And a handkerchief picked up from the lawn."

"Well, my list is n't so very large," said Kathie, with comforting gayety.

But Freddy's list outswelled Rob's. He was quite delighted to regain his lost treasures, some of which had been found in most unheard-of places.

The second week Rob showed a decided improvement. Three articles only had gone astray, while Kathie numbered as many, but the third week he increased to seven, and Kathie had none. For the month his amount was twenty, Kathie's five, and one would think that Freddy had lost the whole contents of his play-house.

"So you see, even at the low fine of a penny, I have fifty-two cents. Fred is the greatest sufferer. I am afraid it will make him bankrupt."

"I think we ought to help him out," said Kathie. "I 'll pay ten cents."

Rob looked grave. It would be rather mean not to offer ten also, but he had only a stipulated sum per month, while Kathie was not restricted.

Uncle Robert took Freddy up on his knee. "My little man," he said, "let the playthings alone a moment, for I want to talk to you. Through your carelessness you have left all these around in the wrong places, and you see they litter up the rooms considerably. If some had remained out of doors, they would have been ruined. Now I want to teach you carefulness. You will have to pay a penny for every one, which will make twenty-seven pennies. As you have but fifty in all, you see it makes quite a hole in your fortune."

Freddy sniffed a little, and began to pick some tears out of the corner of his eyes.

"O, that's no way. You must learn to remember; a boy of eight is large enough, I am sure."

"But I *can't*," he replied, despairingly.

"Well, you can try. You do not forget to come to your meals, or if you are promised any indulgence that never slips out of your mind. I do not like the habit of children laying their books or playthings about anywhere, and even if you make a little improvement every month, it is so much gained. Now Kathie has very kindly offered to pay ten cents of your fine, but I shall not allow her to do it next month."

"And I suppose I ought to pay ten," said Rob, slowly.

While his uncle had been talking he had studied Rob's face as well, and saw the struggle.

"Rob," he said, pleasantly, "you are not compelled to pay anything, and you ought to have the courage to give just the sum you think you can afford. If it was a starving child the case would be different. Now think again and tell us just how you feel about it."

Rob's face flushed, and his first impulse was to say, magnanimously, "Ten cents"; but when he saw the kind and appreciative look in his uncle's eyes he reconsidered. "I'll tell you the truth, Uncle Robert. I'd rather give the ten cents than to have you think me mean; but it seems to me that I can only afford five; that will take my spending-money for this week."

"And that is about right, I fancy. Kathie has the most money, and so she is really not any guide

for you ; besides, I want you to learn to decide such
matters according to your own judgment, and not
take any other person for your standard. It depends
altogether upon the motive whether one is mean or
not. Now, Freddy, I think they have been very
kind to you. You will only have to pay twelve
cents. Get your money."

So they all handed over the fifty-two cents, in-
wardly resolving that the sum should not be as much
the next month. Freddy took nearly a basketful of
redeemed property up to his play-house, and they
saw nothing of him until supper was ready.

"How did school go to-day?" asked Uncle
Robert.

"O, I suppose I shall like it. Mr. Barlow was so
easy, only once in a while when the boys made him
real mad, and for the most part you could do about
as you liked ; but Mr. Crittenden and Mr. Deane are
pretty sharp. I 'm going to begin with Latin. Charlie Darrell is put in the same classes."

It made the Academy much better for Rob after
Mr. Darrell concluded to send Charlie.

"And Charlie is almost a year younger than you,"
said Kathie.

"O, he has the knack of learning; it comes natural to him."

"Then the boys to whom it does not come natural must make the greater effort," replied his uncle.

Rob got on very well, though. In a week's time he had made troops of friends, and by dint of hard studying and some help kept his place; but he did love to play, and the confinement after so royal a vacation was doubly irksome.

In the mean while Kathie and her mamma were making preparations for Aunt Ruth's journey. Kathie was to be housekeeper during their absence. She was to look after Fred and keep him in order, see that Rob did not transgress the bounds of propriety, write every other day to New York, and in any difficulty ask advice.

"After all, it will be real hard to have you go," said Kathie, caressing Aunt Ruth.

"You will be lonesome, but Uncle Robert may be able to return in a few days."

"Not that altogether; I was thinking of you and what you will have to suffer. I wonder if it will be very painful."

"I am to take ether for the worst, you know

The getting well will be quite tedious, I suppose."

"You don't feel afraid, Aunt Ruth, that — anything will happen?"

Kathie's bright face was shaded very sorrowfully, and her clear voice trembled a little.

"My darling, do you mean dying? Dr. Markham thinks there is comparatively no danger. And then one has to trust God always. You know our lives are in his hand."

"Aunt Ruth, are you sorry that I wished it? I never thought of the pain and suffering that night when we were all so happy, only that if you could be well again and walk about."

"My dear child, I shall always be glad that one of your first desires in prosperity was for my welfare. And it will give me better courage to bear the pain, as I think of the comfort that we shall take together afterward"; and Aunt Ruth kissed the tender face.

"When will Dr. Markham let you come back to Cedarwood?"

"He thought in about three months."

"By Christmas! How delightful that will be! We will have a Christmas feast. And if you should be well — But, O Aunt Ruth, sometimes doctors fail, do they not ? "

Aunt Ruth smiled. " Kathie," she said, " I 'm not going to have you conjuring up giants. So far as human eyes can see, the affair promises well. When I am gone you must not worry about the thousand things that may happen. I 'll leave you a text to meditate upon at such times : ' Commit thy ways unto the Lord, and he will bring it to pass.' "

" Yes, that is the best," returned Kathie, cheerily.

Mrs. Alston felt quite anxious about leaving the children, but Hannah was so trustworthy, and Uncle Robert expected to be going backwards and forwards, so she thought that nothing very alarming could happen without their hearing of it soon. Still she gave Kathie many charges, and begged Rob to be as careful as he could, and not increase Kathie's cares.

Then the packing commenced. There was an abundance of easy wrappers, and a good warm double-gown, a pair of slippers that Kathie had embroidered, and rolls of old linen for bandages. Freddy was very anxious that she should take something of his, and even generously proposed his locomotive and his

small music-box that regaled one with Hail Columbia
and Yankee Doodle.

"I am very much obliged," Aunt Ruth replied,
"but you know that I shall have to keep very quiet,
so you had better enjoy these things yourself. And
if you will be a good boy while I am away!"

"I'll be just as good as I can hold," said Freddy,
swelling up and turning red in the face with his resolve.

The trunk was strapped and taken out on the
porch. Mrs. Alston was dressed in a pretty brown
travelling suit, and Uncle Robert was up in Aunt
Ruth's room, ready to assist her down stairs.
Kathie could n't help thinking how lonesome it
would be in this pleasant place after they were gone,
and most of all in the evening, the time of quiet,
comforting talks. She tried hard to wink away the
tears that *would* come, and keep her voice steady.

"I shall be back on Saturday," Uncle Robert, announced, in his cheery fashion, "and I shall expect you
to have a grand supper for me. Now, Aunt Ruth,
think how frisky you will be this time next year.
Why, we shall have you dancing out on the lawn!"

Kathie smiled at that, though, after all, no one

beside the ponies seemed in very gay spirits. Mrs. Alston kissed the children silently, but Aunt Ruth realized the most truly what the parting was to Kathie. Ever since she could remember, Aunt Ruth had been such a dear friend.

Uncle Robert deposited her in the carriage; then mamma was put in.

"Hurrah!" shouted Rob. "Three wishes for success! Here, we ought to have a slipper to throw for good luck!"

"Take mine"; and Hannah pulled off hers.

Rob threw it ahead of the carriage. "Better than we expect," he declared, running after it.

Aunt Ruth leaned out and smiled. That made Kathie quite light-hearted.

"And now we must hurry off to school," said Rob to Freddy, who was sitting on the door-step, hardly knowing whether to cry or not.

CHAPTER IV.

KATHIE'S HOUSEKEEPING.

KATHIE found the morning unusually long, it must be confessed. She took care of the articles that had been left around in the hurry of departure, put her own room in order, and looked out her books, as she meant to study her lessons just the same. But somehow she found it dull music, and her thoughts would wander to the travellers. So presently she took up her drawing. She was making a copy of a picture for Lucy Gardiner's birthday.

The sun shone very brightly, and the air was so warm that she had her window open. Now and then a bird twittered on a tree near by, and she glanced up, her eyes lingering long over the lovely landscape. If she were only a bird!

" This will never do," she said at length, and went to work in good earnest. The factory bell in the village rang for twelve. In a little more than two hours Rob would be home. Freddy took his lunch to school, as he did not return until three.

But Kathie grew tired and went down to the kitchen. Hannah was canning some tomatoes, and this interested her a good deal.

"I should think it would be lonesome for you, Miss Kathie," said Hannah. "I don't know how in the world we shall get along without your mamma."

Kathie sighed. There was a ring at the door-bell, and Hannah was holding a ladleful of tomato in one hand, and a can in the other.

"I'll go," the child said.

To her great surprise as she opened the door, there stood Miss Jessie.

"O," she exclaimed, "I am so glad to see you! I was so lonesome that I had to go down to the kitchen. Will you come to my room and take off your hat?"

"Yes, I came to stay awhile. I promised your mamma that I would look in upon you. What have you been doing, — drawing?"

"I was trying, but I did n't get along very well."

"Your foliage is rather stiff, but otherwise I think

it quite fair. I did not know that you had such a taste for drawing."

"Uncle Robert has been giving me lessons."

"Well, suppose I give you one?"

"O, if you will, Miss Jessie."

Kathie took her seat and Miss Jessie overlooked her, making a suggestion pleasantly, — here a little deeper shading, there more graceful and flowing lines, and soft touches that were such an improvement that Kathie was delighted. She was going on bravely when Rob came home.

"What a short hour!" she said, with a smile; "and the rest have been so long."

"And what a house without mother and Aunt Ruth!" Rob exclaimed. "As you have Miss Jessie, I think I'll go off to the woods with the boys. Duncan set a squirrel-trap this morning."

"O Rob, I hope they will not catch any. Don't you think it cruel, Miss Jessie?"

Rob laughed and called her chicken-hearted. It did n't hurt the squirrels a bit.

"Boys seem to be very fond of the amusement," Miss Jessie replied. "Charlie's pet squirrel was caught in the woods."

"I don't see how he ever became so tame."

"He was very shy and wild at first, but we all petted him a good deal. And yet it never appeared quite right to me to shut up such things in a cage."

"But you let Dick run all over!"

"We do now. I hardly believe he would stay in the woods. He starts when he hears any of our voices."

"I think I should like to have a pet," said Kathie, slowly. "Freddy's rabbits are very nice, but I have n't even a kitten."

"How would you like a canary-bird?"

"If one could tame him and teach him tricks, it would be charming. Your little Cherry is so cunning!"

"One of the young birds, Gypsy, is very wise and amusing. If you think you would like to have him, I will give him to you. But he will need attention every day."

"I believe I should, Miss Jessie."

Fred came thumping up the stairs. "O dear!" he said, "I 'm half starved!" and with that his books went down on Kathie's table, spilling the water out of a vase of flowers.

Kathie tried to check him, but it was too late.
She wiped the water up with a towel, and gently reminded Freddy that this was not the place for his
books.

"But I 'm so hungry!"

"And this is not the kitchen. Hannah will give
you something to eat. Take your books with you
and put them on the closet shelf."

Freddy was gone about ten minutes. Then he
wondered if they could n't go to drive? He was
sure Rob would n't want the horses.

"Will you, Miss Jessie?"

"Yes;" it would be very pleasant, she fancied.

So Kathie sent Fred to order the horses. She put
away her drawing and made herself ready, but they
waited moment after moment, and no Fred and no
carriage.

"If you don't mind I 'll go and see what has happened"; and Kathie ran down stairs.

There seemed to be no stir of any kind around the
carriage-house, so Kathie tied on her broad-brimmed
sea-side and hurried to the Lodge, as she descried
two small figures under a shady tree.

"O," exclaimed Freddy, as she approached, "look

at our windmills! Hooray!"—with a long emphasis of enjoyment.

The two children had some paper stars pinned loosely on a stick, so that when they ran against the wind the stars whirled round in a delightfully entertaining fashion. Grandmother Morrison had made them for Jamie.

"Fred, did you do your errand?"

"O, I did n't want to go riding; I 'd rather stay and play with windmills," returned Freddy, with supreme indifference.

Kathie felt as if she could give him a good shaking. She restrained her impulse of vexation, however, and said, quietly, "Don't you want to go?"

"No, don't be bothering me!" with boyish loftiness, and with that he took a good race across the greensward.

Kathie ran down to the evergreens, where Mr. Morrison was busy, and preferred her request. In a few moments the carriage was ready, and she and Miss Jessie stepped in and drove quite rapidly down the avenue. They had a very pleasant time, and on coming back Miss Jessie asked to be left at her own house.

"I thought you were going to take tea with me," said Kathie, rather disappointed at this proposal.

"I should have to go home immediately afterward, as I have an engagement for the evening; but if you would like to have me come to tea to-morrow I will do that."

"Yes, I should," said Kathie.

As she was going to the house she found Fred on the porch crying. "You were real mean to go out without me"; and his voice broke into rather unmusical "boo-hoo." "I never can go anywhere! Uncle Robert said you might take me out."

"But you told me that you did not want to go," Kathie replied, quite firmly.

"I did want to go afterward, and you might ha' waited."

"Freddy, I could n't. You had your choice, and now you must not cry."

"And Hannah won't give me any supper!"—which was followed by another prolonged wail. Fred had played himself tired, and was rather sleepy and cross

"Where 's Rob?"

"I don't know; I guess the bears have eat him up, or he 's been drownded."

Kathie laughed, as much at the lugubrious accents as the melancholy supposition.

The supper was on the table, but they waited a long while for Rob, and then sat down without him. When they were about half through he made his appearance.

"Why, what made you stay so long?" asked Kathie.

"We went farther than I expected," he replied, briefly. He did not think it necessary to tell her that they had been down to the woods, from thence to the river, and taken a long row.

After supper Kathie put Fred to bed, and Rob tried to study his lessons, but he was too tired and sleepy, so he thought he would take a little nap upon the lounge. The result was that he slept until after nine, and Kathie had hard work to wake him up, and get him off to his own room.

"O dear!" she said to Hannah, with a sigh, " children are a bother and trouble, — are n't they?"

"If they trouble you too much, miss, turn them over to me. Your uncle won't like you to be worried with them," was Hannah's rejoinder, and the good creature meant it to be a comfort.

Kathie felt very dreary and forlorn as she laid her head upon the pillow. What would it be never to have a mamma or an Aunt Ruth again? There were many little girls in the world who had neither, and she prayed softly that God would spare them both for long, long years.

On the whole Kathie's second day was rather better. It was not a particularly bright one to Rob. He missed one lesson, and his exercise was so full of mistakes that he had to stay in after hours and rewrite it. He found Kathie commencing her letter to mamma.

"You need n't blab about last night," he said. "It was an accident. I did n't mean to stay out so late, and I shall not do it again."

Kathie's account was very pleasant in the main, but she confessed that she should be real glad to have Uncle Robert home again.

On Friday they had a delightful letter from the travellers. They were domesticated very comfortably indeed, and found Dr. Markham a refined and courteous gentleman. Aunt Ruth put in a long postscript. Nothing was said about the operation, however, and Kathie resolved that it would not be until the next week.

Uncle Robert started by an early train, and was home at one on Saturday. The children were all delighted. Even Rob, who thought it a grand thing to have his liberty the first few days, began to feel almost as lonesome as Robinson Crusoe on his island.

Kathie brought some lunch in the dining-room, Hannah being very busy. She poured the tea and arranged the dessert as prettily as an older person could have done it.

"How do you like being the head of the house, Kathie?" asked her uncle.

"Not *very* much," she answered, slowly.

"I suppose the boys have been good, and not increased your cares?"

"Yes," said Fred, "we helped her all we could. I carried the weeds out of the path, and cut two bouquets."

"And obeyed her when she told you to do what you did not like?"

Fred looked rather sober over this.

"I am glad to have such a good account of you. One can do a good deal when one tries."

"I'm afraid I did n't *try* very much," said Rob,

and he seemed suddenly to realize that he might have
made it more pleasant.

"How was that?"

"I suppose I did n't think."

"Would you have thought if Hannah had forgotten your breakfast some morning?"

Both boys laughed at this.

"How funny it would be," said Kathie, "if servants
and mothers *should* forget! If you did n't have any
meals or any clean clothes!"

"And it sometimes disappoints the servants and
mothers just as much when the children forget."

"I believe I have n't been *very* good," exclaimed
Freddy, with a lengthened visage. "I forgot about
the horse one day and went to play with Jamie. He
had the most splendid windmills you ever saw, and
then —"

"Well, what then?"

"I cried because Kathie went without me.'

"But you said you did not want to go, Freddy."

"I did n't just then, but I did afterwards."

"Everybody cannot wait for little boys, you know,"
said his uncle. "It was right for Kathie to go if you
told her that, and losing the ride was sufficient
punishment."

Rob thought of his discredit and the missed lesson. It was an ugly fact against him that would come out presently.

But they had a very pleasant time at the table, and then they took a walk through the grounds to see what Hugh had been doing. Everything had been neglected for so long, that although there was a gardener beside Hugh, still the work did not make very rapid progress. It would take another season to bring the place to perfect order.

Then Kathie showed him her drawing, which she had finished, and the lessons she had learned.

"I said them all to Hannah, to be sure that I knew them. But it was n't half as nice as having you at home. Miss Jessie came over every day, and I went out a little."

"You have done very well indeed. I am pleased with your perseverance, for I know it must have been rather dull work."

By this time they had strayed round to Aunt Ruth's room. "Now I want you to tell me all about mamma," she said. "I'd like to hear what they did every day. After you reached New York you took a carriage and went to Dr. Markham's — O, and have you seen Mr. Meredith?"

"Yes, he came that evening. You want it all in the fashion of The House that Jack built?"

"I am not particular about *every* repetition," she returned, amused at the idea.

So Uncle Robert related the main incidents. One had been very pleasant, and that was a call from Mrs. Havens. She had met Mrs. Alston several times during her early married life, and was very well acquainted with her husband's family.

"And she is so very sweet and friendly. Of course mamma liked her. Well, what did they do · on Friday morning?"

"There was a consultation between Dr. Markham and another physician," said Uncle Robert, slowly. "Aunt Ruth had recovered from the fatigue of her journey, so they decided that it would be well to have the operation very soon."   .

"Not then?" exclaimed Kathie, turning white, and grasping Uncle Robert's hand.

"My dear child, it was then, and it is all over. Aunt Ruth is comfortable, though the case was worse, or rather more difficult, than they expected. Don't look so frightened. They gave her some ether, and she went to sleep like a baby. It affected her beautifully, they said. Once she roused a little and they gave her more, and when she came back to consciousness she was bandaged and lying on the bed, and had experienced scarcely a pain."

"O, how good it was that she did not feel it at all!" and Kathie drew a long, relieved breath. "When does the doctor think she will get well?"

"Not in a long while. The most tiresome part is yet to come; but we will all keep of good courage. Dr. Markham thinks that she will only be a very little lame."

"O," exclaimed Kathie, "won't it be royal to have her walking about like other people? And how did mamma feel after it was through?"

"Quite rejoiced, you may be sure. We were in the next room, waiting very anxiously, and were most thankful when the verdict proved so favorable. That part is all through, and we need not think of it any more. On Monday we shall have a telegram. Now, my little girl, don't conjure up any dreadful things."

"O, indeed, I shall not, Uncle Robert. I am so very, very thankful and glad that I did not know anything about it until it was all through."

Uncle Robert amused them in the evening with some old Australian stories that the boys were always delighted with. It was so nice to have him home once more.

"I wonder how we ever did without you," she exclaimed, laughingly, tangling his curly hair with her fingers; "it seems to me that we could n't live at all now."

"Not with your experience of housekeeping, my wise little woman?"

"O, I 've done more than that sometimes," said Kathie; "I 've made cake and biscuits, and I used to sweep the house for mamma; but Hannah would not let me sweep yesterday for fear that it might make my hands hard," — and she laughed gayly.

"We 'll have biscuits for breakfast on Monday morning of your own make, Miss Kathie," Uncle Robert returned; "and now you must all go to bed, for to-morrow will be Sunday, and we must go to church and give thanks."

Kathie kissed him many, many times.

CHAPTER V.

GOING TO A PARTY.

THEIR telegram on Monday contained no bad news. Uncle Robert decided that he would not go to the city that week unless the accounts were worse. Kathie was very glad, but Rob felt that he must be a trifle more circumspect. Of course, the discredit mark came out; but as Kathie had said nothing about his long stay in the woods he concluded that it would be very childish to go into all the details; he was too large a boy to be called to an account for everything.

"I am sorry that it should happen so soon," said his uncle; "I wanted you to have as clean a record as Charlie Darrell."

"O, I can't be as good as that," declared Rob, rather disdainfully.

"I never heard of any boys that were too good," returned his uncle, with a queer little smile.

The event of the week to Kathie was Lucy Gar-

6

diner's birthday party. Mr. Morrison, who was very
ingenious, had made a pretty black walnut frame for
Kathie's picture, and it was polished with oil until
it looked rich and smooth.

"It is n't as pretty as mine," she said, "but it will
look real nice in their bedroom. And, Uncle Robert,
they have a set of book-shelves ornamented with cone
work, which they did all themselves. When Christmas comes I want to give them both a book."

"Your Fortunatus's purse will be pretty severely
drawn upon about that time, I fancy. You had
better begin your list, so that you will not forget
anything."

"A good idea," said Kathie.

Rob thought first that a little girls' party would
n't be of much account, and he did n't believe he
cared to go. But Kathie had heard Annie Gardiner
express a particular desire that Rob should be there.

"I wish you would," she said. "It will seem quite
like old times to see the school children again. We
used to have such good fun with them all, you
know."

"But we really don't belong to that set," he returned. "If it was Dick Grayson —"

"O Rob! we ought not to think the less of people because they are poor. The Gardiners are richer than we used to be, and have a pretty parlor."

"It is n't that exactly, but I don't go to the old school, and — the thing will be a kind of bore. I 'm tired of those foolish little plays. You always have to kiss some one whom you don't like."

"Then you can retaliate by kissing the one you love best," she answered, roguishly. "Rob, I 'm sorry you 're getting to be a big boy. I like little boys the best who believe in lots of fun."

"My fun is different," he said, loftily.

In truth Rob was feeling of considerable consequence. All the changes had conduced to this. The fact that he was living in one of the handsomest houses in town and had a rich uncle exalted him in the eyes of many boys. Then the Academy pupils were of the so-called "better class," and more than one thought it looked quite grand to sneer at poverty as something rather disgraceful. I 'm glad to say that Dick Grayson did not do it, and Charlie Darrell would have been much above such a feeling. Rob had a peculiar sensitiveness to what any one said, as if the people who are continually making disparaging

remarks were not the ones to whom the least attention should be paid. But some boys, and a good
many girls, are fearful they will not be estimated at
their full value if they do not proclaim it in some
especial manner.

The party at the Gardiners' was a wonderful thing
to the two girls. Their mother had entirely recovered, and was as well and rosy as before,— one of
those genial, good-natured women who make every
one happy that can be reached by their influence.
Annie and Lucy had been very devoted through their
mother's illness, and in casting about for some reward
she had thought of this entertainment.

"I don't believe very much in children's parties,"
Mr. Gardiner said. "If they could come and have a
little cake and fruit, and some wholesome fun, I
would n't mind; but children nowadays have as
much to say as their elders, and we can't afford such
doings as they had over to Cedarwood."

"And they would be the last to approve of us
if we did. I mean a pleasant, simple affair that will
not prove expensive, and the girls will think so much
of it. They were compelled to give up a good many
pleasures in the summer."

"Very well," said Mr. Gardiner, "do as you like."

So when she asked the girls what they would like most of all, Annie said a party. They were wild with delight when they found their mamma was in earnest. They helped all they could, picked over dried fruit, stoned raisins and beat eggs, for they were quite serviceable cooks already.

Kathie was made happy by a good long letter from her mamma, in which she said that Aunt Ruth was doing the best they could expect, and was quite comfortable. Then on the morning of the party Uncle Robert had a great box of flowers cut and sent over to the Gardiners.

"How delightful of you!" Kathie said, smiling from her soft eyes down to the very tip of her rosy chin.

Rob stood on the porch with his books strapped together. Kathie thought that he did n't look very bright, and with her usual generous impulse wondered if she could do anything to please him. Perhaps he did *not* care to go to the party. She would be sorry, but —

"Rob," she exclaimed, "did I tease you too much the other day about going? It would be pleasanter, but if you 'd rather not — "

"O, I'll go," said Rob, with sudden decision.

"Do you want anything fixed to-day that I can do? And I'm so glad!"

"No, I believe not," he answered, slowly, yet he lingered as if all had not been said.

Kathie studied his face. It was rather uneasy and wistful. "Dear Rob," she began, "I wish I could do something for you."

"You can, Kathie," ·hesitatingly and with an effort. "I hate to ask it of you, but —"

"What is it? You know I'd do anything, Rob, — that was right," she added, in a lower tone.

"O, there's nothing wrong about this," he spoke up more bravely. "I wish you'd lend me twenty-five cents until Uncle Robert gives me mine on Monday."

"With pleasure," returned Kathie, and she ran swiftly up stairs to her little store.

Uncle Robert had given Fred fifty cents a month, and Rob a dollar, for any small expenses they might have from time to time. They were to receive it weekly, and not to ask their mother or Kathie for any more spending-money. But this was only borrowing.

Kathie came down with a beaming face. Of course Rob must be rather short, for in the beginning he had to pay the fine on his stray articles. And since he had pleased her about the party she would do any kindness for him.

She squeezed it softly into his hand and kissed him. He felt much relieved, and would have gone to half a dozen parties, he thought.

All the day Kathie was as merry as a lark, but she did not forget her lessons, nor some sewing she had taken in hand. And while she sewed Uncle Robert read a very entertaining child's history aloud to her, questioning her afterward concerning the principal events. She progressed as rapidly with her studies as if she had been in school.

Miss Jessie had sent her bird over, and she found it a great deal of company. It was a very pretty canary, quite deep in color, with a tiny black crest on the top of its head, and a little black tuft that it was fond of pulling out so that it could droop over its wing. Kathie used to laugh at this proceeding.

Gypsy would wash, pick out his feathers and oil them until they shone, and last of all pull the black ones until they were in the most conspicuous place.

and then march up and down the perch as if he
thought himself exceedingly fine. He was a magnificent singer, though he had but recently begun, for he
was only a little over a year old.

"But, after all, nothing can make amends for
mamma and Aunt Ruth," Kathie declared. "So you
will have to tell me whether I am nice and party-
like, Uncle Robert."

He thought she looked very pretty in her white
dress and blue sash. Rob returned home in good
spirits, and as Annie had charged them to come
early, they did not loiter until an ultra-fashionable
hour. Indeed, they were nearly the first, but Kathie
did n't mind that, and as Rob and Mr. Gardiner
compared notes on ponies, he felt quite well entertained.

They did have a good time. Sophie Dorrance had
gone to boarding-school, and Lottie Thorne was at her
aunt's, and some of the boys seemed to have grown
so much since the night they frolicked at Charlie
Darrell's. But they played ever so many amusing
games, and danced Sir Roger de Coverley, and then
came the refreshments.

Mrs. Gardiner's wide kitchen had been scrubbed

until it shone. The table was spread its full length, and graced by two lovely pyramids of flowers. There was the grand iced cake in the middle, and different varieties at each end, and great dishes of the most luscious peaches and pears and grapes. Then on a side-table were slices of watermelon, crisp and rosy, and as the evening was warm the children enjoyed it wonderfully. The fruit they had of their own, and as Mrs. Gardiner said afterward, "it could n't have been any nicer if they had spent a month's wages upon it."

But the funniest of all was a play they had afterward called Adventures. The children took a slip of paper and wrote first the date of any year, then any kind of a house, any sort of business, a place, a relative's name, a sum of money, the name of a town or country, any sight, an article of any kind, and then any sort of deed that any one might do. After this the papers were collected, though I should say each child's name was signed to the paper.

Mr. Gardiner was to read them. The first was Kathie's. He had a little outline on a card, and the blanks were to be filled in with what the children had written.

"Here is Miss Kathie Alston's adventures," he announced.

"Miss Kathie Alston was born in the year fourteen hundred and ninety-two," — at which the children all smiled, — "in a log-cabin on the prairie, and followed shelling peas for a living. At the island of St. Helena she met her grandmother, who gave her six cents and told her to travel round the world and enjoy herself." Here the half-suppressed merriment became so audible that it broke into open laughter.

"Think of travelling round the world for six cents!" whispered Charlie Darrell.

"Well, she went to China, and saw the man in the moon, and bought an elephant. When she returned home she put on the teakettle and made tea."

"What did you do with your elephant?" some one asked, and "Whom did you invite to tea?"

"But your grandmother wasn't very generous," declared Lucy Gardiner.

So when they had laughed and asked her all the questions they could think of, Mr. Gardiner prepared to read another.

"Master Charlie Darrell was born on Fourth of July morning, eighteen hundred and sixty, at Westminster Abbey, and followed shoemaking for a liv-

ing.   At the extreme north of Greenland he met
his brother, who gave him fifty thousand dollars and
told him to travel all round the world and enjoy
himself.   He went to Dublin and bought a fish-
ing-pole.   When he returned home he pulled off
his shoes and drowned himself in the Atlantic
Ocean."

"A tragic ending, I must confess," laughed Kathie.

Some of them were very amusing indeed.   Rob had
a million of dollars, with which he bought a quart
of peanuts; and one little girl had twenty dollars,
with which she bought a crying baby.   And they
went to nearly every corner of the world, while
some of them were mere children and others hun-
dreds of years old.

It was quite late after this was through, and
they began to disperse.

"We've all had such a delightful time," said
Kathie.   "I've enjoyed everything and laughed
until I actually ache all over.   What fun it has
been!"

"I'm so glad!" replied Annie.   "Of course it
was n't anything like your party."

"That was everybody's party," said Rob, "and I think this has been fully as nice, according."

"And you are sure you have enjoyed yourself?"

"O, famously!"

Annie was delighted with this praise, and took great comfort in repeating it to her mother.

"There could n't have been anything that would have made me as happy," she said.

"And I 've always wanted a party," rejoined Lucy. "O, it 's been splendid, but I 'm tired and sleepy."

"And your clean floor 's a sight with watermelon seeds and cake-crumbs," exclaimed Patty Brown, who had come in to help.

"We 'll sweep them up and not mind for once," said Mrs. Gardiner. "It 's time we were all in bed."

Kathie had to stop and tell Uncle Robert a little about the party, and Rob confessed that he had enjoyed himself first-rate.

On Saturday, to the great delight of the children, Mr. Meredith made his appearance. The day before he had seen Mrs. Alston, and Aunt Ruth was doing finely. Mrs. Alston sent much love to them all, and a little note to Kathie, which the child enjoyed greatly.

They had so many new things to show him. First he must go and see Fred's rabbits, which he pronounced exceedingly pretty.

"Are you making a collection of such purely orna- mental creatures ?" he asked, with a smile.

"I 've collected two," said Fred, proudly ; "and a house, but Rob made that, only I helped him *some*."

"I know a man in New York who has some cunning little guinea-pigs that he would like to sell. Now, if you could get a house for them, I might send them down."

"O," exclaimed Kathie, "would n't they be lovely !"

"How much will they cost ? I don't have but ten cents a week," Freddy said, slowly.

"I believe I will send them to you on condition that you take very good care of them."

"Won't I have lots of things !" and Freddy danced round with joy. "I 'll be sure to feed them every day."

"And I have a bird," said Kathie, "the sweet-

est little fellow alive, and he sings beautifully."

"I heard him the first thing as I entered the
house. Do you train him to give your visitors
such a welcome?"

Kathie laughed. "I hung him in Aunt Ruth's
room because it seemed so lonesome in there.
Miss Jessie gave him to me."

"Are you as much in love as ever?"

Kathie looked puzzled a moment, then a bright
light broke over her face. "Do you call that being
in love?" she asked.

"Yes, I thought it quite a positive case."

"I do love her very, very much; and Uncle Robert likes her too."

A peculiar look came into Mr. Meredith's eyes.
Kathie wondered what it could mean, but it was
quite beyond her youthful capacity.

Just before sunset they took a drive, and stopped
for Miss Jessie, bringing her over to supper, and
they had quite a gay time. Kathie was complimented upon her success in pouring tea, and they
all concluded that she made quite a notable housekeeper.

"Yet I can't help but think, in nearly everything, that we should be so much happier if mamma were only here."

Amid her quiet watches and long, uneventful hours her little daughter's love was a great comfort to Mrs. Alston. Kathie never wearied of writing letters; and she filled them with the simple details of every-day life, so that it seemed almost like looking in upon them.

Kathie was very sorry to have Mr. Meredith return so soon; but he said it was only a flying visit, to see if she had cried herself into a shadow, and when she came to New York they would have rare times indeed. His brother's family were to move in town the first of November, and there would be Ada, very glad to see her also.

Rob paid his debt to Kathie very promptly; but in two days he borrowed again. She longed very much to give him the trifling sum, and when he was compelled to go through the same process the next week, she said, thoughtfully, "Rob, suppose I ask uncle if I can't give it to you? I don't believe he would care."

"No," returned Rob, "you must not say a word

about it. I mean to be real economical next week, and I know that I can get up straight; but it seems hard to have only twenty-five cents a week. Why, there 's one boy — Lu Simonds — who spent a dollar yesterday. I would n't mind if we were poor."

" But we are not rich, you know. It is all Uncle Robert's money."

" All the boys know that he has plenty. I hate to be thought mean and stingy ! "

" What do the boys have to buy ? "

The question was so sudden that Rob colored in spite of his effort at indifference.

" O, there are a good many little things. Girls cannot understand very well."

" I think I can," said Kathie, with the kindest-hearted pertinacity, " if you only would tell me ! "

" Well, suppose some time Lucy Gardiner or Mary Cox did something real nice for you; would you not want to — to — make some kind of return ? "

" Why, yes," replied Kathie, with alacrity.

" Well, that 's just the way of it. Some of the boys are clever to me, and I hate to be shabby in return."

" But there are a good many things that one can

do — " without money, Kathie was about to say ; then she checked herself, feeling that after all there might be a little in her brother's perplexity that she could not understand. She was so frank and honest that she could not readily take in any specious reasoning.

But when Rob wanted to borrow another quarter before the week had ended, she thought there must be some difficulty, and was a little worried herself. What could she do to help him out of it ? Would it be very wrong to give him half a dollar, and *not* tell Uncle Robert? She might put it down in her book of expenses as simply a gift.

That course did n't look right and true to her. She had learned the lesson which seemed so difficult for Rob to acquire, that it was so much easier to tell anything in the beginning. This kind of burden grew so rapidly, and what appeared only a very small matter at first became like a mountain after a while.

So one crisp, bright morning, as she and Uncle Robert were taking a pleasant drive, she summoned up courage to open the subject very delicately, she thought. Uncle Robert had been mentioning two or three charming little gifts that it was in her power to bestow.

7

"Don't you think," said Kathie, soberly, "that you are too — too good — indulgent, I mean, to me?"

"Have you been forfeiting my confidence, and does your conscience trouble you?"

But there was such a merry twinkle in his eye that Kathie saw he was n't a bit afraid.

"I shall have to balance your accounts to see if you have been embezzling."

"No," returned Kathie. "I have n't done anything, I was only thinking — "

At this Uncle Robert laughed outright, and Kathie joined him when she caught the merry sound.

"It was n't of myself, or not altogether. I was thinking that I could spend money any time, and Rob had — such — a very little."

This seemed real ungrateful to Kathie. A year ago a dollar a month, all her own, would have been a fortune to her.

"Has Rob been complaining?"

"No"; and Kathie colored slightly, wondering if what Rob had said could be justly termed complaining.

"Do you think he ought to have more to waste upon candies, or nuts, or boyish indulgences? You know he is not required to buy so much as a pencil, or any needful article, no matter how slight."

"Uncle Robert," she said, slowly, "what do you suppose boys buy generally?"

"A great deal of useless trash. They certainly have enough to eat and drink at home, but the temptation of spending before other boys is very great. I am inclined to think that Rob would be very lavish and wasteful if he had plenty, yet I want him to have a few lessons in the art of spending money. However, I fancy his allowance is large enough for the present."

There was no hope, then, in this quarter. She could n't help feeling a little sorry.

"You look disappointed, Kathie."

"Do I?" and she tried to smile.

"Kathie," Uncle Robert began, kindly, "was this altogether an idea of your own, or did it arise from something that has been said to you?"

Poor Kathie! she had made a sad mess of it. If she told the truth Rob would be in trouble, and she could not answer wrongly.

"If you please, Uncle Robert, I would rather not —" and Kathie's lip quivered a little.

"My child, you are not compelled to tell me. While it is pleasant to have all your confidence, I still wish you to feel quite free."

"You have all *mine*." Then she turned away her face that he might not see the tears that seemed to flood her eyes without dropping. But he knew they were there, Kathie!

They were silent for several moments, and when Kathie felt her voice steady and clear she said, softly, "Uncle Robert, please forget all about this. I ought not to have said a word. You are very good to us both."

But Uncle Robert felt that there had been a little rough place, and though he was anxious to know, he very wisely forbore to question her further, as he thought it just as necessary for children to honor one another's confidence as for grown people. And then Kathie was such a sweet little darling that he would not have subjected her to any pain.

CHAPTER VI.

GETTING OUT OF DEBT.

UNCLE ROBERT cast about for several days to discover some feasible plan for learning the state of his nephew's finances, but none seemed to present itself, and his patience was abundant. He had suggested that Rob should keep accounts, but Rob could n't bother.

It came out very oddly, though. The month of October began on Monday, and Rob received his allowance in the morning. He was half a dollar in arrears, so he gave his money to Kathie, rather reluctantly, it must be confessed, yet he tried to say cheerfully, " I mean to be real economical this week, if I possibly can."

In the evening Uncle Robert announced that there were some articles in the pound, though he was pleased to find the number quite small. Kathie had two, Rob seven, and Freddy ten. Kathie very promptly paid her amount, and Freddy handed over his.

"I'm afraid I can't redeem mine to-night," said Rob, in an off-hand manner, much entertained with the click that his knife made as he opened and shut it.

"No trust," returned his uncle, laughingly. "I know you had some money this morning."

He colored and could not resist looking at Kathie, who blushed as well.

"Kathie, you have n't borrowed his money, — have you?"

"No," she said, rather faintly.

Uncle Robert looked as if he wanted an explanation. Rob could not brave out the steady gaze.

"I owed her," he said. "I had borrowed some the week before."

"And do you owe her anything now?"

The question was asked very pleasantly, but it made Rob cross. The whole thing would have to come out. He almost imagined that Kathie had been telling.

"Yes," he answered, very reluctantly.

"How much?"

"Twenty-five cents."

"I'll lend you some," offered Freddy, kindly.

" No, my boy. As a general thing it is not good policy to borrow even to pay debts. Take your play-things up stairs. I think you can see by the hall lamp. And it is about your bedtime."

" Won't you go too, Kathie ? " with a very wistful look.

Kathie sprang up and relieved his small hands of a part of their burden.

" Now for it," thought Rob, secretly kicking the leg of the table.

" Rob," his uncle began, quietly, " how did you come to get so much in debt during the month ? "

" I don't know," impatiently.

" If you had kept accounts as I asked you, you could tell easily. It would be a guide for your next month's expenses, for on glancing it over you might omit the foolish and unnecessary items. I wish you to do it next month."

" If I can't spend a cent as I want to, I might as well be without," was the angry reply.

" As I do not know how you have spent it, I can make no objections at present. But if you prefer you can relinquish it."

" The other boys have lots of money."

" Who are they ? "

" Why, Dick Grayson and Lu Simonds and Walter Ray."

" Do they spend it in the same manner ? "

" Why — yes. "

This was not exactly true. Dick Grayson was an exception.

" Then you must know what it goes for, Rob ? "

Rob hung his head, and determined upon an obstinate silence.

" Have you bought books, paper, or pencils ? "

" No," after a long pause.

" Rob," said his uncle, with a peculiar smile, " I mean you to answer my question if you stay here all night. It will be no harder now than an hour hence. If it is anything you are ashamed of, tell it out bravely and have done with it ; if not, why hesitate ? "

" The other boys do the same," he replied, crossly.

" Now we are talking of what you did. How have you come to spend fifty cents more than your allowance ? "

Rob was silent. His uncle took up a book to make the lengthening moments seem less awkward. Presently Kathie entered, fancying the matter had

A VERY QUIET TIME.　Page 105.

been amicably settled in her absence. Uncle Robert kissed her with grave tenderness. "My darling," he whispered, " I am going to dismiss you for this evening. Amuse yourself in the best manner that you can."

Kathie went out quietly, wishing with all her heart that she could bring Rob to her way of thinking; but Rob much preferred his own will.

To a third person the silence would have become absolutely laughable. The clock struck nine, at length, and Rob was growing sleepy from the enforced quiet. He supposed he would have to tell. It was hard that he never could have any fun like other boys, but that he must always be treated like a baby, as if he did n't know anything, or have any wants; and every pulse swelled with indignation. This government was worse than his mother's.

He made a desperate effort. Rising, he went almost past his uncle, and, without looking at him, said, in no very amiable tone, " I 'll tell you how it was; the boys treated me and I hated to be mean, so I could n't help but treat in return."

Then he would have left the room, but Uncle Robert clasped his arm gently. " I supposed that it was something like this," he returned, in a clear, encouraging manner; "sit down and let us talk it all over. What were the treats?"

But Rob had made his effort, and now relapsed into sullenness. "Soda-water and creams," he said, after another pause, "and nuts and oranges."

"Because you were hungry or thirsty?"

"Well, the other boys do it."

"My dear boy, I wish you felt in a better mood. This is one of the temptations that I knew would befall you. I consider it a foolish and useless practice, and one that leads to a great deal of harm; but boys and men are always exposed to it at some time during their lives, and perhaps it is less difficult to break when one is young. Now, do all the boys treat, or only a part of them, — Charlie Darrell, for instance, or Dick Grayson, and those who are really high-toned and studious?"

Lu Simonds was one of the worst boys in school, and yet one of the best-natured. His father was rich and indulgent, and Lu thought it looked rather grand to spend lots of money, even if he rarely had a correct lesson. Several of these boys had taken a great fancy to Rob. He was so gay and amusing, so ready for any kind of fun. Yet the association was rather dangerous for a boy of his temperament, and he had a secret consciousness that Uncle Robert would not altogether approve of his companions.

" Is it the best and noblest boys in school who do this, Rob ? "

" They 're well enough, I suppose."

" I am afraid they are not ; and this treating is a bad habit that I want you to correct. I would much rather have you do it for yourself than from any compulsion."

Rob made no answer.

" Possibly you may think me strict about it, or ' grannified ' as boys say ; but I want to feel that when the time comes you can be safely trusted away from home for your mother's sake. I want to see you a brave, honest, truthful boy. You must do what is right without thinking what this one or that one will say. It is a hard thing, I know. Boys make mistakes and so do men, but I firmly believe that if the boys were trained to have more strength, the men would not fall into so many errors. Have you anything more to tell me about it ? "

Rob was not a bit penitent. He was sorry and

ashamed at being forced, as it were, to confess, but he thought it very hard to be called to an account for every little thing.

"I 've told you all," he said, shortly.

Uncle Robert had meant to forgive the debt and let him start fair again, but the tone was so very unpromising that he changed his mind.

"And what do you propose to do?"

"O, I 'll pay Kathie; I told her I would," he answered, loftily.

"And then resolve not to borrow any more for pleasure. We all have to learn these things by experience."

"Good night," said Rob, coldly, leaving the room.

Uncle Robert sighed. This was so different from Kathie's frankness and love. Freddy was less stubborn, though he did not retain any impression permanently, yet much of this was due to his childishness. Rob had some fine, sturdy qualities if the right ones could only keep the ascendency and rule.

In his own room he felt that he could do as he liked, so he flung his coat on the first chair and kicked his slippers half across the room. As that did not restore his mental equilibrium, he gave vent to a flood of angry tears.   A boy of almost fifteen to be treated like a baby!   Uncle Robert might keep his money, and Kathie hers, he would n't touch another penny if — if he was starving, he pretty nearly said.   Then he wondered how they would feel if he ran away and went to sea.   He used to think that would be a gay life, and anything would be better than this tyranny.   I am sorry to say that he hurried through with his prayers, for he did not exactly dare to go to sleep without repeating them, and he soon sobbed himself to forgetfulness.

He was rather quiet the next morning and cross to Freddy, but his anger unwittingly gave him courage for one good move.   After school the boys had a game of ball, and of course they played until they were tired and hungry.   Just beyond the green there was a confectionery, the place of temptation for them. It had a small saloon attached, where one could obtain almost any kind of refreshments.

"Come," exclaimed Lu Simonds, "let's go in and have some oysters.   They 'll taste good after this hard work.   I 'll stand treat."

Two of the boys started with alacrity, but Rob hung back.

"Come, Alston, don't be fussy!"

"No, I cannot."

"Why, that's funny! You're not often counted out when the good things are going round."

Rob's face was scarlet.

"I shall have to be after this," he said.

"Why? Do they disagree with you? Or have you grown delicate?"

Rob turned fairly round, though he little guessed what a brave deed he was about to undertake.

"Boys,"— and there was a great lump in his throat that almost choked him, — "I can't treat any more myself, and I'm not shabby enough to take anything that I can't return."

"Has the governor shut down on you?" asked Lu.

"Yes."

"Come along, it will not make a bit of difference. Only it's mighty hard for you, and awful mean, I say."

"And he has lots of tin! He's a precious miser, Alston, but maybe he will leave you a big pile in the end," said the elegant Walter.

"Good night, boys"; and with that Rob turned away abruptly.

"I hope they 're satisfied," he muttered, with tears of mortification in his eyes, the *they* meaning Kathie and Uncle Robert. "No, I 'll never take a cent again, and I was bound that the boys should know just why. It 's real mean and hateful."

Rob was a little glum for several days, it must be confessed. They all treated him exactly the same at home, as if, indeed, they saw no difference in him. The boys renewed their invitations, and offered him anything that chanced to be going round, but he steadily refused. He did not notice that every time it came easier.

And so the next Monday morning when he received his quarter, he turned it over to Kathie at once. He was still too sore to have any discussion about it, but he was thawing out a little.

As he was going in the school-room he met Mr. Crittenden. A rather stern-faced yet not unkindly man, holding the boys in check more by awe than love.

"Good morning, Master Alston," he said, pleasantly. "I was glad to find a marked improvement in your recitations last week. I began to think you were falling off rather fast. You ought to be a good scholar, for you look like a boy who has work in him."

Rob had been in that desperate state where hard study was a relief, and yet now he did feel pleased to be thus complimented. It made him resolve to study this week. He *had* fallen into careless habits, or rather his habits of application had never been very remarkable.

He wanted very much to tell Uncle Robert, and he really could not keep it from Kathie. She was so delighted that she repeated it immediately. Uncle Robert did not mean to ask for any confidence, yet he was deeply pained by its being withheld. A stranger would hardly have noticed the reserve, but these little things are keenly felt by those who love.

Ah, children, do you ever think how often you give pain to your best and dearest friends in this manner? Household confidence and freedom are so sweet that coldness and reserve seem grievous in the place. And though this pride may appear a grand armor to the one who is wearing it in some fit of anger or disdain, remember how it would be regretted if death should come between! What if you should never be able to express your love again, and find the lips that might have kissed yours cold and still!

The news from New York was still very favorable. Mrs. Alston expected to return in the course of a week or two, and though they had become quite used to her absence, they were delighted with the prospect of having her back. Aunt Ruth was confined to her bed yet, as Dr. Markham did not think it safe for her to attempt sitting up.

"I wonder if she will want me?" Kathie asked, thoughtfully. "I only wish she could come home with mamma."

"I shall miss you very much if it is considered best for you to go. You are a great comfort, little girl."

"Am I?" and Kathie kissed him fondly, but there was a peculiar wistfulness in her soft eyes.

"Uncle Robert," she said, some time afterward, "don't you think we might forgive Rob the rest of the debt? I am afraid he isn't very happy, and then he doesn't have a penny for anything."

"I 'm not sure, Pussy, but that it will be best to let Rob fight out his battle alone, as he seems to desire no interference. I think he will come around right in the end."

This gratified Kathie extremely. The fall was

8

very pleasant, and they had many nice drives and rambles through the woods. Uncle Robert procured some large rustic baskets, and helped Kathie to fill them with flowers and mosses. Two were to be kept in Aunt Ruth's room.

"And we might have a jar of ivy standing here ; it will run up beside the window and look very pretty."

" O do," exclaimed Kathie, eagerly. " I want this place to look just as lovely as it can when Aunt Ruth comes back."

So they found a large urn-shaped jar and put in not only the ivy, but some scarlet geranium and tufts of tropical grass.

"Why, the room begins to look like a conservatory!" declared Kathie, with joy.

"There are so many entertaining things that one might do, my little worker. I was thinking how nice it would be to have a collection of autumn leaves."

"O, can't we ? " asked Kathie, pleadingly. " I 've saved ever so many."

" They want to be pressed very nicely, and varnished with the thinnest coating we can give them.

Then we might get a portfolio and arrange them on the pages. In this manner one can look at them without tumbling them over, and they will last a long while."

Even Rob was interested in the collection, and brought them home some very beautiful specimens. On Saturday morning they all went to the woods and had a gay time gathering nuts and leaves. Rob was quite like himself and in the best of spirits.

In the afternoon several girls came over to see Kathie. Uncle Robert asked his nephew if he did not want to help him varnish the leaves, and Rob went at it with much interest. They had a very brilliant collection in mingled scarlet, gold, crimson, and brown. They were laid on a smooth board to dry, and were to be left there over Sunday. Afterward Rob washed his hands and changed his clothes, and then he did not know exactly what to do with himself. Uncle Robert found him sauntering around the library.

"Rob," he said, cheerily, "you have not had any money for so long that I believe I shall give you your allowance to-day."

Rob drew back rather haughtily. He had resolved

all along that he would not take any more money,
but he remembered that he still owed seven cents,
so there was quite a struggle between pride and
justice.

"I owe you seven cents for the mislaid articles,"
he answered, huskily, "and — I don't want the rest."

"Why, Rob! Do you get along better without
money?"

Rob's lip quivered a little, and he averted his
eyes for a moment; but one of those sudden and
irrepressible impulses seized him, and he glanced
up in spite of himself.

"Rob," said his uncle, in a very winning tone,
"let us forgive and forget, and be good friends."

Somehow Rob could n't help thinking of the first
night of joy at his uncle's return, and his stubborn
courage gave way. He winked very hard to keep
the tears out of his eyes.

"My boy, you have been fighting a rather severe
battle alone"; and his uncle's hand was laid softly
upon his shoulder, and how it was he could never
exactly tell, but he hid his face in the little nook
made by the protecting arm, and actually cried.

"Rob," his uncle began, in a low tone, "I have

suffered too by being shut out of your confidence for the last two weeks. Suppose we try again. I did not mean to be as severe to you as you have been to yourself."

And so they clasped hands in token of reconciliation, but it was some moments before Rob was calm.

"I suppose it did seem hard, but I have a fancy that the discipline has been productive of some good. The first week you were at school your record was perfect, and it has not been since, until the past fortnight. But I want you to try the money again. I think it better that a boy should be able to face temptation than always be kept out of it."

Rob was thinking. The first week it had been a sore trial, and every day he had felt angry and mortified, but of late he had hardly remarked it. He had not gone quite so much with Luther Simonds's party, and he believed that was the reason his deportment had been better, and his scholarship more perfect.

"You don't say a word, Rob. Do you not care to be friends?"

"O Uncle Robert, it was n't that. Yes, I 'm very glad"; and his voice choked up again.

"Then we will begin anew. The old debt shall
be forgiven, and we will start fair."

There was something so frank and cheery in his
uncle's tone that Rob's heart warmed to a very
tender love.

"I did n't mean not to take any more money because I was better without it, but — "

"Because you felt too proud."

"How did you know?" and Rob glanced up eagerly.

His uncle smiled. "That was no great mystery.
After one has studied people for a good many years
one can guess pretty correctly."

"I did n't like to be thought the worst boy in the
world," said Rob, "though I 'm bad enough"; which
was quite an admission for him.

"No one entertained such an idea."

"I wish I could be good, but I don't believe I ever
can. It does n't come natural to me as it does to
Kathie."

"We all have to try, I believe. In two weeks
you have made some improvement."

"Uncle Robert, it was n't for the sake of being
good"; and there was a strand of penitence in the
boy's tone.

"But you might try next time for the sake of being good."

Rob sighed. Instead of being a martyr and a hero, as he had fancied himself, many of his motives looked very poor and unworthy.

"Now suppose we finish the afternoon and our talk by going to drive," proposed his uncle, who thought that a change of scene might conduce to a still further confidence.

In this he was right. By degrees Rob went over his late experience with much clearer eyes. He even admitted that the system of treating was not a good one, for, beside spending the money foolishly, it made some of the poorer ones feel very uncomfortable because they could not join in the indulgence. "I don't believe I shall ever do it again," he said, thoughtfully.

Rob was not one to make great professions of penitence and forget them the next day. He was thoughtless and careless, to be sure, but there were some good, strong elements in his character. As a boy, he would never be the favorite with girls that Charlie Darrell was, yet he might mature into as noble and good a man.

Uncle Robert was striving earnestly to do his duty by all these dear ones that he had taken in charge. His own experience had been peculiar and varied, and the height to which he was striving to attain for himself was that of a Christian gentleman. He had his trials, too, for we are none of us exempt; and few who had known the gay, rollicking Robert Conover of fifteen years before, always as intent upon his own pleasures as Rob was now, would have looked for the patience and self-denial and tender thoughtfulness that had become his leading characteristics; but with him, too, it had been a hard fight.

CHAPTER VII.

JUST IN LUCK.

ROB came home from school the following Monday with a look of peculiar satisfaction upon his face. He made a rush through the house to find his uncle, and discovered him helping Kathie to put the finishing touches to their collection of autumn leaves. They were tastefully arranged, and made a series of brilliant and interesting pictures.

"And, O, there's some news!" exclaimed Kathie. "We have had letters, and mamma wants to come home this week. Uncle Robert will have to go to New York to-morrow."

"I'm glad about mamma; she has been away five weeks; but I think we have done pretty well, — all but the first week," he added, as an after-thought.

"And this week will be lonesome again," said Kathie, disconsolately.

"Why, I thought you were going to be brave," Uncle Robert said, with a laugh.

"Well, so I am; I was n't complaining exactly.

"We shall all miss you,—more than we did at first, I think," confessed Rob.

"It 's a wonder to me how we ever lived without you," said Kathie, with her arch, mirthful look. "Now these are all arranged. Where shall we keep our portfolio ? "

"In the library, I suppose; that is the place for our intellectual matters."

"And this is strictly intellectual," added Kathie, laughing; "I 'll go put it in its place."

"Well, what is it, Rob ? " asked his uncle; "you have something to tell me, I fancy."

"Yes,"—and Rob smiled at being so readily understood; "it 's about school. We had quite a time to-day, and I 'm so glad—"

"About what ? "

"That I have not had any money for two weeks, though my virtue came from necessity; for if there had n't been that time about it I suppose I should have borrowed again and spent *some*."

"And what is the cause of rejoicing ? "

"Why, just before we were dismissed to-day Mr. Crittenden told us that a matter had come to his knowledge, which he should be compelled to investigate, though it was not strictly school business. And then he went on to say that there had been a system of treating established in the school; and, though he did not object to any boy's sharing his luxuries with another, this had assumed such serious proportions that the father of one of his pupils had called upon him to interfere. The boys had been in the habit of going to Watson's, and some of them had ordered more than they were able to pay for. Two bills — one of five dollars and a half and one of seven — had been sent in to parents; and the boys, in excuse, had said that nearly every one in the school treated, and they did n't want to be called mean or stingy. Then he asked all the boys who had treated for the last two weeks to rise."

"And you were not among them ?"

Rob colored warmly. "I was *so* glad; but, Uncle Robert, out of thirty-nine boys only eleven kept their seats."

"I think it is high time, then, that the practice was stopped."

"Mr. Crittenden talked pretty sharply, though he said he should not punish any of the boys then, but that in future it must not be considered any habit of the school, and if such a story came to him again the offenders would be made to regret it. He read them a lecture upon spending money foolishly and running in debt, and I felt that it was all meant for me, although I was not standing up. So it's a lucky thing that you found out"; and Rob flushed again.

"A bad habit can never be discovered too soon. I confess that I was a little afraid that you might run in debt."

"There never would have been any chance of paying it"; and Rob could laugh at the absurdity. "But those poor fellows looked pretty cheap, I tell you. I'm thankful that I wasn't among them."

"That is better than any volume of sermons that I could have delivered," said Uncle Robert; "now you see its practical working."

"I was pretty mad at first," confessed Rob; "but I'm thankful now, and I guess I have learned a lesson."

Kathie had stopped to arrange some books, and now made her appearance, so the subject was dropped, and mamma's return taken up. Uncle Robert was to start to-morrow morning, and come back probably on Thursday.

"That will only be three days," exclaimed Kathie, "and then we shall see dear, dear mamma! I can hardly wait."

Freddy made a great rejoicing also. To be sure he had experienced many ups and downs, but that was Freddy's lot generally, and on the whole Uncle Robert had made a very good mother. Still, home was not quite the same place when deprived of its loving centre.

So they kissed Uncle Robert and sent ever so many loving messages to mamma and Aunt Ruth. And they did very well during the three days, being gladdened with a telegram informing them in what train they might expect the travellers.

"I'm glad they will not get in until five," exclaimed Rob, "for now I can go to the station with you. I tell you, there 'll be a gay time!"

But Kathie thought of poor Aunt Ruth alone, and how very solitary she would feel. She was quite willing then to relinquish all her pleasures at home and go to the invalid.

The family carriage was taken out, and the children set off in high glee. Of course they were there nearly half an hour before the train could be expected, and they were quite sure that some accident had happened. They counted every moment and every second, listened for the sound through the cedar woods, and at last heard the distant whistle.

I believe there never was quite such a sweet sight to them as mamma's face, a little paler and thinner for her confinement to the sick-room, but the soft, tender eyes were undimmed, and the kisses as warm and fond as absence and love could make them. They quite forgot about Aunt Ruth in this overwhelming joy.

"I want to sit by mamma," announced Fred.

"Yes, you shall. I suppose you have been a good boy all this long while ?"

"The goodest you ever saw,"—with sublime disregard for his order of comparison. "But, mamma, I believe my locomotive is in pound"; and he gave a suspicious glance at Uncle Robert. "I 'm pretty sure — that I — took it up stairs — the last time I had it."

"It would be wonderful if it had run away," said his mother, smilingly.

Kathie sat on the same seat and held mamma's hand. She was so glad to have her back again! Almost six weeks — And yet, what if one should have no mamma!

The air was quite keen, so they drove briskly homeward. Hannah had a warm welcome for her mistress, and there was a tempting supper on the table.

"I made the cake and the jelly," said Kathie; "and now you are tired, I know, so I'll pour the tea, for I have become quite used to it. And we will have a nice talk about all you have been doing."

It proved rather an account of the children's "doings," — how Freddy had two such beautiful guinea-pigs, and some little rabbits, the cunningest that you ever saw, and Kathie had a bird that sang from morning till night, and now if they could only have a parrot!

"Ah, Freddy, I am afraid there will always be something," said his mother.

It seemed as if they never would get talked out. Fred begged to sit up a teeny little while longer, and was sure that the clock only struck seven when it was eight. But Kathie was quite relieved when the

little chatterbox had made his exit, and they could
have mamma to themselves.

Aunt Ruth was improving as rapidly as could be
expected. She sat up a little each day in a peculiar
sort of reclining-chair made for such cases, but even
at the best she could not attempt to walk before
another month.

"If she only *can* come home by Christmas," said
Kathie. "I keep thinking all the time what a lovely Christmas we shall have. Two months only to
wait!"

"I hope it may be delightful, but it seems to me
that nothing can be pleasanter than coming home to
such a lovely place and such dear children."

Mamma's smile was certainly the sweetest thing
in the whole world.

At last she sighed as if she might be tired, and
Uncle Robert declared that it was high time for them
all to be in bed.

"I shall have to get up at the peep of day and go
to studying," declared Rob. "The only thing I've
done has been to write my translation."

"Mamma," Kathie said, beseechingly, "I think I'd
like to come and sleep with you to-night."

"And I was just going to ask you. I have not seen my little girl for so long that she is very precious to me. And I am afraid that I shall have to part with her soon, but we will not think of that to-night."

"I 've been happy a good many times," said Kathie as she cuddled in her mother's fond arms, "but now I am full of thankfulness and content to the very brim."

The next morning Mrs. Alston unpacked her trunk. There were a number of new dresses for Kathie that must be made immediately, for Aunt Ruth wanted her as soon as she would be ready to come.

"She does n't need a nurse now, but some one to do little errands and wait upon her, and you are so used to that. And Uncle Robert has been making arrangements for you to take lessons in music; so this, with a practice every day, will give you a walk. Mr. Meredith was very anxious that you should come and recite with his brother's little girl, but we concluded that would be rather too much."

"O, did you see Ada?"

"Yes. I have met her twice only. Mr. Meredith

9

is very fond of her, and I believe she is quite accomplished."

That was all Mrs. Alston said. She did not admire Ada altogether, but neither did she desire that Kathie should be prejudiced or acquire habits of unkind criticism. She thought that she could safely trust her little girl even to adverse influence for so short a time.

"I'm glad that I can study music. Miss Jessie has been giving me a few lessons, and I like it so much. I suppose we shall have a piano."

"Some time," answered her mother, quietly. She knew that it was to be Kathie's Christmas gift, but it was a secret as yet.

They went out to find a dressmaker, and though Miss Latimer was very busy, she promised to give them two days and do the fitting, and to have a seamstress at the same time would expedite matters.

"How odd it seems to be looking for people to come and work for us!" said Kathie, gayly. "I sometimes almost forget who I am."

Mrs. Alston found it quite a relief. She had spent a good deal of her time during the past six weeks in sewing, and active exercise was a pleasant change.

And so Miss Latimer came and cut and talked. She appeared to know about everybody, and all the clothes they had worn for the last seven years. She was very pleasant, however, and not ill-natured in her gossip, though she did say at her next place, which happened to be the Thornes', "Half a dozen dresses, and not a single silk among 'em! The child going to New York too, where she 'll be asked out to parties. I would let her have something like other girls in her station, if I was her mother!"

Kathie thought them especially pretty, — a cloth dress trimmed with scarlet, and a waterproof with a scarlet hood, a beautiful bright plaid poplin, and some soft merinos. The green one was made with a dainty zouave; the blue, almost the color of her Cinderella dress, as she called it, was embroidered with black braid, her mother's work during the long watches; and then the lovely rose crimson, which seemed the prettiest of all, if there could be any choice.

"Kathie," her mother said, "it is Aunt Ruth's fancy to have you come, for she is so accustomed to your ways. Dr. Markham did not quite approve of it at first, as he thought it too confining; but when the arrangements were made he acquiesced, though he reserved the right of sending you home if he found it was likely to injure your health. I expect you will be lonesome at first, and if you get homesick you need not be afraid to write. I do not want you to stay if you are not contented."

"But I think I ought to be," replied Kathie, "and with Aunt Ruth too!"

"Two months will be quite a long stay, though likely you will come home during that time. But I have said this so that you might feel sure we should not be disappointed if you desired a change, or think it a crime."

"Mamma, I shall be very sorry to leave *you*," Kathie answered, gravely. "But it will be pleasant for Aunt Ruth, and that must be my comfort when I feel a little down-hearted, — if I should."

The bright face promised a most cheerful companion, and yet it was not an easy thing to go among strangers when she loved them all so well at home.

But Rob thought that all the nice things came to her. Two days would have finished him out, had it happened right for him to try the experiment.

Kathie went to Mrs. Gardiner's to take tea, and to Miss Jessie's. The latter was coming to the city to spend a fortnight with some cousins, and altogether the prospect did not look very alarming. Kathie kept up a brave heart, though she did have two or three quiet cries when she was all alone at the thought of parting with mamma.

Uncle Robert treated it as a pleasant visit, and it would have been quite impossible to get low-spirited. So she said her good-bys cheerfully, and they were whirled to the city as fast as the great iron horse could take them.

Aunt Ruth was delighted to see them. Kathie was a little shocked at the change. She had seen her when she had been pale and thin, but now her complexion was transparent, and all the tiny blue veins had come to the surface. Her eyes had a peculiar, wistful look, and the tears came into them as she kissed Kathie.

"My little darling," she said, with deep emotion, "I cannot tell how glad I am to see you. Your coming is like sunshine to me."

At that Kathie felt repaid for the sacrifice.

"I suppose you are getting well?" she asked, hesitatingly.

"O yes, but it is so very slow"; and Aunt Ruth sighed.

"Are you sorry that I wished it?" Kathie's soft lips murmured against Aunt Ruth's cheek.

"My precious child, no. It is very tiresome to be sure, but I think of the delight we shall have when I am well. And I have longed to see you so. Now that you have come I shall be content."

The past ten or twelve days had been very lonely for Aunt Ruth. She had suffered a good deal and was weak and nervous, and longed for a familiar face. For so many years she had been the centre of the household, listening to childish cares and griefs, and sharing every one's pleasures. The utter deprivation of interest, and the enforced quiet had worn upon her spirits, that were usually so cheerful.

Dr. Markham eyed Kathie with a trifle of suspicion, yet his voice was pleasant as he asked, "Do you think you can play nurse, little one?"

"Yes," answered Kathie, "if any one will tell me just what to do."

What a bright, winsome face the child had, to be sure, and such a soft, low voice!

"O, there's nothing to do, that's the worst of it. And keeping still is not very entertaining to young people."

Aunt Ruth smiled at Kathie, as if they two could enjoy quiet moments, even if much talking was forbidden.

Presently Uncle Robert left them to go to his hotel, and Dr. Markham, after giving a few orders, went down to attend to a new patient. Kathie had time then to take a survey of the place.

A large back room in the third story, with a prospect that was not very enchanting, it must be confessed, as you could see nothing but the rear of the houses in the next street. It was very pretty and pleasant inside, however. A little fire was burning in the low grate, and it gave the green carpet a cheerful glow, while the flowered chintz curtains at the window were suggestive of sunshine; a tiny centre-table with a vase of flowers, and no untidy bottles or cups standing round. Just beyond was a smaller apartment containing a single bed.

"I suppose this is to be mine," said Kathie, smilingly. "Did you have a nurse after mamma went away?"

"There is another patient, and as we are neither of us in a critical condition one nurse answered very well for both. But when one has to lie in bed helpless it is so nice to have some one of your own. I missed mamma so much.

"I am very glad that I have come," Kathie said, in her sweet, cheerful tone. "And you need not be afraid that I shall get tired or — or homesick."

"O, I mean that you shall go home now and then. I don't want to be selfish with you."

After Kathie had finished her tour of inspection she drew the low rocker beside Aunt Ruth's bed, and took the wasted hand softly in hers.

"Shall I talk to you?" she asked, "or will it hurt you?"

"No, I think not. I am not strong enough to do much of it myself"; and Aunt Ruth gave a faint smile. "Tell me all about Cedarwood. It seems as if I had been away a year."

Kathie was very entertaining indeed. She told of all the pleasant things that had happened, the party at Mrs. Gardiner's, and was just coming to their collection of autumn leaves when Mrs. Markham entered. She was a pale, high-bred looking woman past fifty, but so sweet that Kathie was won at once.

"Why, you are actually looking improved," she said to Aunt Ruth. "Are you sure that you have not talked yourself into a fever?"

"O, I have been listening principally."

She laid her hand softly on Aunt Ruth's brow, and found it moist and tranquil.

"It has been rather lonesome for her," said Mrs. Markham. "It is not quite as if she were too ill to see any one, and after a month or so the bed begins to grow wearisome. But she has been very patient."

After getting a little acquainted with Kathie she took her down stairs for supper. The nurse was to bring Aunt Ruth's, and then she was to be left quiet for an hour or two.

Kathie felt rather afraid of Dr. Markham at first. He had a habit of giving sudden sharp looks that almost startled her, and he asked odd, abrupt questions; but before they had risen from the table Mr. Meredith came in, and presently Uncle Robert joined them. Mr. Meredith teased her a little about playing nurse, and declared that he meant to get sick the first time he came to Cedarwood.

Kathie found the next day that her duties would not be very arduous. She dusted the room, and after Aunt Ruth was taken up, combed her soft hair in the gentlest manner. Then she read to her a little, and waited upon her whenever she wanted anything. In the afternoon Uncle Robert came to take her out, and explained to her about the music lessons. A Mrs. Gifford was to give them twice a week, and every day Kathie was to go and practise two hours if she could.

"And that will be sufficient for you to have on your mind," said Uncle Robert. "It will give you a good walk and make a pleasant change.

They went to see Mrs. Gifford, a little roly-poly woman with a face full of smiles and dimples, and a soft, rich voice that was music itself.

"I am sure I shall like it," said Kathie, delightedly. "Why, I don't believe that I shall feel a bit homesick."

Afterward they called on Ada Meredith. They were ushered into an elegant parlor, and the little lady came to receive them in her most gracious manner. Kathie had a feeling of astonishment, and she was not quite sure that she liked so much grandeur. The children were out with their nurse, but Kathie could not forget them, and left fond messages for them all.

CHAPTER VIII.

PLAYING NURSE.

AFTER seeing Kathie nicely domesticated at Dr. Markham's, Uncle Robert returned home. The boys had bemoaned him sadly, Fred especially, who made daily lamentations concerning his locomotive, which he was quite sure had strayed into pound in spite of his carefulness.

Aunt Ruth was certainly improving. I think part of it was due to Kathie's cheerful presence and the charming way in which she anticipated every want. Mrs. Markham declared that she was a treasure, and the doctor petted her in numerous quiet ways, now and then indulging her in a drive. She did possess a very sweet and happy nature ; but it was not that alone. She was trying to grow a little better every day. She had temptations like all other children, and she did not always feel patient and self-denying ; but she remembered the war upon the giants, and that she was not to give it up until she had slain some of them.

She often thought of the happy home at Cedar-wood, and mamma, and talked about them all to Aunt Ruth. November was very dull and rainy, and the cheerless-looking houses opposite were not as pretty as the long rows of evergreens and the broad, beautiful lake; but sometimes she amused herself with a group of children, who seemed to make a nursery of one room, and an old lady by another window, who appeared to be always darning stockings.

She soon began to give Aunt Ruth her meals, and when her appetite was not very sharp she used to coax her, and sometimes feed her as they had Rob when he was sick. She was so neat and handy that the nurse thought it a marvel.

"I never saw such a child!" she would exclaim. "She is like a little woman. Why, where did you learn it all?"

"I suppose it is because I 've had to work," Kathie replied, smilingly; "when we did n't keep any servant I always helped mamma."

"But you are a born nurse, certainly."

Aunt Ruth looked gratified at this commendation. Kathie certainly was the dearest little girl in the world.

It was odd, perhaps, but Kathie thought her music the greatest trial of all. She was very fond of it, but she wanted a tune instead of the exercise or fingering that must go over and over again, until she felt that she could fly away from the sound. She had a very quick ear, and could catch the air of almost any tune. Now and then she used to indulge herself, or improvise some little melody; but one day Mrs. Gifford said, "Miss Kathie, that may be a very pleasant break in the practising, but I do not like to have you do it; it takes your attention away from the lesson."

Kathie missed her little pet airs sadly; but when she found her fingers running into the temptation she tried to check it as quickly as possible. One day, when it had seemed more difficult than usual, she went home in a grave mood.

"What is the matter?" Aunt Ruth asked, presently.

Kathie gave her bright, winsome smile, and stirred the coals by way of collecting her thoughts.

"Aunt Ruth," she said, slowly, "I wonder if people ever get to that state where they love to do right always, and when it is no longer hard?"

"Only in heaven, I guess," replied Aunt Ruth,

softly.   "We may love to do right, but so many circumstances arise to make the wrong easiest."

"But it seems to me if any one *could* always think
in time —"

"There seem to be some cases where we really
cannot.   And then you know, if there were nothing
more for which we needed to strive, our life-work
would be done."

"I am afraid we shall never have it done," Kathie
said, rather sadly.

"What is the trouble now?"

"The trouble itself is n't very much"; and Kathie
laughed at it.   "But it is the constant trying, just
as you think you have gained some victory."

"Kathie, that is just what God set us about.
Life is to be a constant trying for something better
than what we have."

"Suppose we don't always love to try, Aunt
Ruth?"

"Then we must pray for grace."

Kathie was silent for many moments.   After
a while she said, "Aunt Ruth, I believe I am getting spoiled.   Everybody praises me until I 'm beginning to feel like skipping the hard things and doing

only the easy ones. And so I shall have to turn over a new leaf."

"Well, you may get a light to see it," returned Aunt Ruth, with a pleasant laugh. "While you can remember as easily as that, you will not go very far out of the way."

"Aunt Ruth," she said, coming to the bedside, "I believe I have n't confessed all. Yesterday, when I was at Ada's, she was having such lovely new dresses made. She went to two parties last week, and an opera, and is going to take part in some tableaux. She had a beautiful bouquet sent her, and — "

"And your life began to look dull, — was that it ?"

"Well, not exactly," said Kathie, "only I stopped to wonder if I should be any happier with all those beautiful things. And yet I don't know but that it was more her way of acting, as though she pitied me a little for not having as much. Still, Aunt Ruth, I am real happy, and I do try to be good."

"And you succeed many, many times, my darling."

Then the tea came up, and they had a pleasant time over it. And afterward Kathie thought of home, which was still the dearest place in the world.

The next morning Mr. Meredith called. A friend had placed an opera-box at his disposal for the evening following, and he proposed that Kathie and Ada should share it.

She flew up stairs to Aunt Ruth. " To think ! " she began, joyfully, "an opera ! The very thing I meant to wish for when Uncle Robert came."

He had treated them to one flying visit already, and was expected again the next week.

" Kathie," Aunt Ruth asked, "would you like to have a new dress ?"

" O no," she said. "Mr. Meredith thinks my crimson merino so pretty, and always calls me little Red Riding-Hood, so I shall wear that."

She was all anticipation until the night came. The opera was to be Il Trovatore, and she begged Aunt Ruth to tell what it would all be like, but it seemed to her, when she reached the place, that no description could do it justice. Their box was like a little parlor, and commanded a view of nearly the whole audience. Such beautiful women and such elegant dresses were new sights to her, then the great chandelier made the place a blaze of light.

Ada wore a blue silk with an overskirt of white tarlatan, and the most exquisite of kid gloves. She was very ladylike, and leaned back on the divan with all the languid grace of a grown woman. But Kathie made a much prettier picture with her bright young face so full of interest and enjoyment. Her soft light curls floated around her shoulders in unrestrained freedom, but Ada thought it more stylish to have her hair rolled and fastened in a glittering bead net which was very fashionable just then. Somehow Kathie did n't envy her a bit, though she had lovely ear-rings and a necklace.

After the music began, she could think of nothing but that. She attempted to follow the English translation, and then let her libretto fall, and listened with her whole soul. The choruses were wonderful to her, and some of the singers' voices were very fine.

Almost at the last, at the close of one of the acts, a very distinguished-looking gentleman entered the box. He was dressed in military costume, and Mr. Meredith called him General. He introduced him to the two girls.

"I 've been watching this one's face for some time,

10

and confess that I half envy your relationship. Her
interest and appreciation has entertained me more
than the play."

He took Kathie's bare, dimpled hand in his as he
spoke, and gave her a most cordial smile.

"O, this is my niece," corrected Mr. Meredith.

Ada bowed in what she considered a very stately
fashion. General Mackenzie looked rather amused,
and Mr. Meredith bit his lip. It seemed to him that
Ada was in a fair way of being spoiled, and improved
rapidly upon it. He had always been very fond of
her, but he could not quite approve of this miniature
woman.

"Do you understand the story?" asked the General, sitting down by Kathie.

"O no! I did read the English a little while, but
I like better to watch their faces and guess from
what they are doing. Some of the music is so very,
very beautiful!" and she drew a long breath.

"Is it your first opera?"

"Yes," she answered, with a bright smile. "I do
not live in the city."

Ada could have checked her frankness. Kathie
certainly had no style or tact.

"Ah, I thought these roses spoke of green fields."

That made the roses deeper. Ada felt rather jealous of the look of admiration and approval.

"You appear to be very fond of music," General Mackenzie said. "I suppose, of course, you play, as all little girls do?"

"I am just beginning."

"Then you have n't come to French songs?"

"I don't know any French at all," said Kathie, innocently. "And I believe I should like the opera better in English; but the orchestra pleases me so much. I like to hear all the instruments."

"And a brass band, how does that suit you?"

Ada was sure that he was laughing at her, and she frowned slightly as a hint to Kathie.

"It makes one think of the war," said Kathie, slowly, "and the brave men who march away joyously, for I suppose they cannot help it, the music is so inspiriting, but afterward —"

"They need it afterward sometimes," the General returned, thoughtfully.

"I have seen one regiment go through Broadway," said Kathie. "They were playing 'Scots wha hae,' and it was beautiful but sad, I thought, though very courageous."

"The old Scots were plucky people. A good cause nearly always makes good soldiers."

"You have been in a battle?" said Kathie, with a little awe in her voice.

"Yes." He uttered the word gravely.

"I wonder if men are not afraid?" she asked, in a low tone.

"My little girl, I suppose some are. But a good soldier, whose trust is stayed upon God, knows that, whether living or dying, it will all be right."

"And you think of him?"

"I try."

Kathie reached out her hand unconsciously. He took it in his and pressed it with fatherly tenderness, then bestowed upon her a look of tender appreciation.

"The curtain is rising," he said, with a smile.

So Kathie turned her attention once more to the stage, but her thoughts wandered to the brave men whose only operas were martial music, and the stage scenes battle array.

There was a great applauding, and then everybody made a rush for the entrances.

"Is your little friend staying with your brother?" asked the General.

" No, at my uncle, Dr. Markham's."

Kathie did not hear the rest, for as she turned to draw on her cloth gloves Ada said, " What a pity you did not wear kid ! No one thinks of going out in the evening without nice gloves."

But Kathie was too happy to be wounded by the remark.

CHAPTER IX.

A GOOD SOLDIER.

AUNT RUTH was much entertained the next day, listening to a rehash of the opera and descriptions of General Mackenzie. Kathie was as happy as a bird, and wrote a long letter to mamma, declaring that she was not a bit homesick. But for all that it would be very delightful to come home, and Christmas was not quite three weeks distant. Then she wondered if Aunt Ruth would be well enough to return to Cedarwood by that time. She had begun to walk a little, to be sure, and yet it did not seem to Kathie that her improvement was very rapid.

"Aunt Ruth," she asked, presently, "do you think you shall be able to go home by Christmas?"

"I hope so, my dear."

That finished the letter joyfully.

Two days after she met Ada as she was returning from her music practice.

"O," exclaimed Ada, with a great deal of importance, "General Mackenzie was at our house yester-day. He is a very distinguished soldier."

"I am sure he is good and brave," Kathie replied, warmly, not at all annoyed by either announcement.

"Mamma desired me to play for him, and he complimented me quite highly."

"That was nice," said Kathie; "I should like to see him also."

"He is going away in a few days. His regiment is at the West."

Ada had felt quite neglected the evening at the opera, and absolutely envious that Kathie should have had all the attention; so now she made the most of her triumph. Her mother was putting her foolishly forward, and she was fast losing the charm of childhood.

"I don't suppose that you will see him," Ada went on. "He is an old friend of papa, and of course he came to our box to see Uncle Edward."

Kathie had no desire to dispute this. Ada's rather ill-natured shaft fell harmless.

But as Kathie was hurrying through the hall at home Mrs. Markham intercepted her. "There is a gentleman in the parlor waiting to see you," she announced, smilingly.

"Mr. Meredith?"

"No."

"O, I know, — Uncle Robert!" and she made a hasty plunge toward the door.

"She is as pretty as a picture in anything," thought Mrs. Markham, so she let her go.

General Mackenzie thought her a very bright picture also. Her waterproof, with its scarlet hood, and a dainty black velvet cap with a tuft of scarlet feathers, framed her in charmingly; but the soft eyes, full of surprise and pleasure, the sweet scarlet lips, and the whole face, so full of health and happiness, was a sight to do one good.

"I could not go away without having another glimpse of you," he said, rising and taking her hand. "I tried to find my friend Meredith; but as I could not I thought I would venture alone, and trust your generosity to excuse an old soldier."

"I am very glad, I am sure," replied Kathie, and there was a ring of welcome in her voice; "but I supposed that it was my Uncle Robert, so if you will please to excuse me I will go and take off my hat and cloak."

She was so simply graceful, without any striving

for effect, that General Mackenzie turned her round and looked her all over with a pleased and curious smile.

"Have you any brothers or sisters?" he asked.

"Two brothers only."

"What do you imagine your papa would say if I ran away with you?"

"I have n't any papa," she answered, gravely; "he died a long while ago."

"And I have n't any little girl. I did have two, but they are dead."

There was a look of grave, sweet pity in Kathie's face, and when she next spoke her tone was low and tender.

She ran up stairs presently, and while she was brushing her hair told Aunt Ruth about General Mackenzie, ending with, "I only wish you could come down and see him."

"I think you will be able to entertain him," said Aunt Ruth, smilingly.

So Kathie went back to her visitor, and they had a delightful time. In a little while they were well enough acquainted for Kathie to tell him how her uncle came home, and the pretty house they had at Cedarwood, and about Rob and Freddy.

"I have a son named Robert," said the General, "but he is nineteen, and a cadet at West Point."

"Then he is learning to be a soldier?"

"Yes, a good soldier, I hope. He is all that I have."

"Then you have n't —" and Kathie paused, coloring a little.

"Well?" with an encouraging smile.

"Any home, I was going to say."

"No, my dear, not in your meaning of the word. But I can imagine what your pretty Cedarwood must be, and all the happy faces that form its circle, and I hope God will spare you a long while to one another. I should like to meet your uncle, but I am going away so soon."

Kathie felt strangely drawn to General Mackenzie, and quite as if she had known him all her life. Yet he was so unlike Uncle Robert or Mr. Meredith, who comprised nearly the range of her gentleman friends. He was very entertaining and related many pleasant little incidents that had come under his observation. He made her laugh, too, with accounts of their life in the different forts, and camping out. She thought how very much Rob would have enjoyed it. Whenever there was anything particularly delightful Kathie always wanted to share it with those she loved.

"I have made you quite a visit," said General Mackenzie, rising. "I do not suppose that I shall see you again, but I shall keep a very sweet remembrance of a little girl who does n't seem at all tired of her childhood, or desirous of outgrowing it. If you retain your truth and simplicity, my dear child, you will make a very lovely woman. God grant that you may!" He stooped and kissed her forehead, and Kathie felt that it was like parting with an old friend.

"I hope you will come back safely," she said, with tears in her eyes.

"And do my duty. That is the wish for a soldier."

It was almost dark by this time, and Kathie ran up stairs again to Aunt Ruth. There was a letter from Uncle Robert awaiting her.

"O," she exclaimed, joyously, "they are coming next Monday,— Uncle Robert and Miss Jessie! And, Aunt Ruth, if we *could* all go home together!"

Aunt Ruth sighed softly and turned her face away. How could she disappoint Kathie in the midst of her rejoicing! — for her trial, alas! was not yet ended.

Kathie read the letter aloud.   They were all so hopeful at home, yet longing to have the break in the circle filled by the two who were still astray.

"Two weeks from next Tuesday will be Christmas," said Kathie as the supper-bell rang.   Then she kissed Aunt Ruth a dozen times, and declared that she was so happy she was afraid that she was not good for much.

"I think I shall have to be looking after you a little more sharply," exclaimed Dr. Markham.   "The idea of having a General spend half the afternoon with you!   Did n't he persuade you to run away and become a soldier?"

"No," returned Kathie, with a grave smile.   "He thinks some soldiers are needed at home."

"Well," said Dr. Markham, "how much courage and endurance have you?   Could you bear a pretty sharp disappointment?"

"Not until after Christmas," Kathie answered, laughing.

She did not notice that he looked rather serious. She was so full of her own pleasant thoughts that just now she could take in nothing beyond.

"Indeed," she said to Aunt Ruth, as she was going

to bed, " I feel so happy that I am almost afraid something will happen to me."

The next day, while she was taking her music lesson, there was a consultation held in Aunt Ruth's room. It was decided that part of the work would have to be done over again, or the recovery would prove less perfect than Dr. Markham desired. This would be nothing in comparison with the former operation, but would, of course, entail a longer period of waiting and convalescence. To refuse would be folly indeed, and yet Aunt Ruth felt much disheartened. To add three more wearisome months to her term of suffering and endurance would prove a hard burden. And she wondered whether Kathie would not be tired with the long stay.

She meant to ask her that evening, and give her the option of returning home ; but just as Kathie had seated herself for a good talk, as she said, the servant came up to announce " Mr. Meredith and General Mackenzie."

" Oh ! " she exclaimed, and yet she was pleased. " General Mackenzie is to go to-morrow. He has come in to say good by again."

True enough. They were passing, and the General

declared that he could not resist the temptation. Besides, he said, they had an important question for her decision.

Kathie looked amused.

" I have been trying to persuade Mr. Meredith that his country needs his services. You remember we were talking of duty yesterday, Miss Kathie."

Kathie had not thought to have it come home to her so soon. The bright face grew suddenly grave.

" Ah, you are not going to desert your colors ! "

" Kathie, tell the General that I cannot be spared " ; and Mr. Meredith looked at her in the most comically entreating fashion.

" The case is this," went on the General, good-naturedly, but with an undercurrent of earnestness. " Here is our friend Meredith, young, in good health, without the nearest family ties, and his country calls all such to her support first."

" But you old campaigners understand the art of war so much better. And, to tell the truth, I may have a strand of cowardice in my nature."

" Does he look like it, Miss Kathie ? "

" No," said Kathie, " it is not that. But it seems hard to go away — "

"Are duties always easy and pleasant?"

"No," with a little quiver in her voice.

"I think his country has need of him. In her peril she has need of all good and true men. And the question is whether he shall stay at home in ease and luxury while others give all, — wealth, the charm of pleasant households, and their own lives."

Mr. Meredith laughed a little. "How solemnly earnest you are!" he said, gayly. "Now, Kathie, my dear child, do you think it is my duty to become a target for a stray ball simply because I am so unfortunate as not to have a wife? Answer truly."

"It is not exactly that, Mr. Meredith, — "

"Ah, Kathie, you are going over to the enemy. I see it in your face. So you want me to join the rabble and march down Broadway to the melodious sound of a solitary fife and drum? You know I can't be a general and go off in state."

"I should not want you to go at all, I'm afraid; but if it was necessary — " and her voice faltered a little.

"You would give me up! Is that my reward, Kathie?"

"No, I should not give you up. I should think of

you daily and pray for you, and believe that God would send you home safely."

"Come," said General Mackenzie, "you have not any excuse. I shall take you to the nearest recruiting-station."

At this moment Mrs. Markham entered, having been detained by some household matters.

Kathie looked very gravely at Mr. Meredith. "Do you really mean to enlist?" she asked.

"Advise me. Would you let your uncle go?"

Her lip quivered with sudden emotion and her eyes filled slowly with tears. "It would break my heart," she said, in a soft, tremulous voice; "but other children have given up their fathers, and I would try to be brave."

"My dear Kathie, it is a shame to tease you," he said, warmly. "Mackenzie is in dead earnest, though; yet I believe I have n't much taste for fighting. How would it do to send a substitute?"

"O, that would be just it!" she answered, much relieved.

"Every man ought to do his duty in such times as these; and if he does not want to go, he can smooth the way for some one who will."

" I am glad you have him converted thus far," said General Mackenzie.

"The credit is not mine," returned Kathie. " He thought of it himself."

Afterward she told him that her uncle and Miss Jessie were to come on Monday. He professed to be surprised, though I think he was not very much.

General Mackenzie looked at his watch and declared they were outstaying their time. So the good-bys were said again.

" You have one quality of a soldier, Miss Kathie, — you face a duty without shirking," were the words he uttered with his parting smile.

It was so late then that after Kathie had read Aunt Ruth kissed her good night ; she went to bed, but she lay awake a long while, wondering if she ever could let Uncle Robert go for a soldier.

The following morning was cold and rainy. When Kathie's duties were ended, she took up a pretty Afghan that she was crocheting for Dr. Markham.

" Kathie," Aunt Ruth said, " I want to talk to you awhile."

Kathie glanced up wonderingly.

11

"I suppose you are counting a good deal upon Christmas at Cedarwood."

"O, so much!" and the tone was extremely eager.

"You have been very good to stay here contentedly and wait upon me."

"It has not been any hardship at all, Aunt Ruth, but just like a pleasant visit."

"I am glad to hear you say so. And can you keep a merry Christmas without me?"

"Without you! Why?" asked Kathie, in surprise. "Will you not be well enough to travel?"

"No, my dear child. The operation has not been quite so successful as Dr. Markham hoped, and a little of it must be done over again. So you see I cannot keep Christmas with the rest of you."

"O Aunt Ruth! I am *so* sorry!"

"My darling, I regret it also. It seems too bad that anything should mar our first happy Christmas at Cedarwood. But you must forget me a little while and enjoy yourself to the utmost."

Kathie did not reply for some moments. It was a very great disappointment. And when she thought of Aunt Ruth all alone while the rest were making merry her heart almost misgave her.

" Will the operation be very painful, Aunt Ruth ? " she asked, in a low tone.

" It is only very slight, I believe, but it will of course delay my recovery. I do not think I should be well enough to go home if that had not happened. You see I cannot walk across the floor yet."

" I wonder if — you ever will be well," — and Kathie's tone was slow and hesitating.

" Dr. Markham thinks so."

Kathie felt that the words were not uttered real hopefully.

" But what do *you* think, Aunt Ruth ? or, at least, what do you feel in your heart ? "

" That it is as God wills, my darling."

Kathie felt a great choking in her throat, and could not speak. It seemed to Aunt Ruth that she really had not strength to say the rest, so she would let it wait. Kathie's stay had been very pleasant thus far, it was true, but it might be duller after the gay holidays. There were other forebodings, too, that she could not quite shake off, — a fear, perhaps, that even this skill and experience could hardly work a miracle.

" Will mamma come down again ? "

" Not for the operation. It is hardly worth while ;

indeed, she will know nothing of it until it is over."

Kathie wanted very much to ask when it would be, but her courage failed. Certainly not until next week, she thought, and then Uncle Robert and Miss Jessie would be here.

There was nothing more said about it, though Kathie tried to be cheerful and talked of General Mackenzie, whom she liked very much. But she was exceedingly tender to Aunt Ruth, arranging her dinner in the most tempting fashion, and coaxing her to eat.

In the afternoon she went for her walk as usual. Mrs. Gifford found her very grave and quiet. She was thinking about her disappointment, and something else, — the possibility of staying on with Aunt Ruth and giving up the Christmas visit. Mamma could not be spared, and even if she were, Cedarwood without her would not be much better than New York. Only last night General Mackenzie had told her that she faced a duty without shirking. Could she when it came to that?

It was still cold and cloudy, although it did not rain. Somehow a peculiar feeling of homesickness came over Kathie, — a longing for mamma and her brothers that filled her eyes with tears and gave her a dreary pain at her heart. She *must* go home, it seemed, if only for a few days.

But then she had coaxed Aunt Ruth to come. Perhaps the latter might have been content with her lameness and difficulty in getting about if she had not set her heart upon a cure, and made it one of her wishes. Yes, it was clearly her duty to stay. So she swallowed a bitter pang and tried to smile bravely, understanding that there were soldiers in common life as well as on the battle-field.

Kathie did not enter at the hall door as usual, but at the area, in order to leave her muddy rubber boots down stairs. Passing the office door quietly, she caught a sentence, in Dr. Markham's voice, that transfixed her with surprise.

" I really did not think she was so weak. She stood the operation very well, but it was as much as we could do to keep life in her afterward. I am afraid she fancies that she never will get well. Somehow, I shall be most sorry to have Kathie go away. The child is so bright and cheerful, and serves to keep up her spirits — "

Just then the door, slightly ajar, was pushed open, and Kathie entered, her face as white as a ghost's.

Dr. Markham uttered an exclamation of surprise, and Mrs. Markham would have caught the child in her arms, but Kathie spoke.

"I could n't help hearing, Dr. Markham, and I know it is about Aunt Ruth. O doctor, will she ever get well?"

"My dear child, physicians are sometimes powerless, or no one would be allowed to die; but it seems quite possible to me that your aunt will recover. Do not distress yourself."

"And you have had — this afternoon —"

"The second operation. The physician who has been here is very sanguine of perfect success, and I feel the same."

Kathie's lip was quivering with intense emotion, and the nervous weakness that makes one want to cry, but she restrained herself bravely.

"It was her wish that you should not be told," the doctor said, kindly, taking the little hand in his. "She thought it would cause you much anxiety, and it could not lessen her suffering, you know. She will be a little worse, or rather weaker, for a few days,

doubtless, but you must be courageous and hopeful." The kindly eyes gave her their most encouraging smile.

"Dr. Markham," she began, slowly, "I shall not
go home at Christmas, or indeed until Aunt Ruth
gets well."

"My brave child! But is it because — "

"No," she interrupted, "I was thinking of it
before. O Dr. Markham, you don't know, but when
Uncle Robert came home he seemed like a prince
from fairy-land, and he gave me three wishes. One
was that Aunt Ruth should be cured. The pain
and suffering did n't come into my mind then. I
only thought how splendid it would be to have her
walk around like other people, and enjoy all the
delightful things in the world, for we had never been
rich before. So it is right that I should stay with
her instead of going away for my own pleasure. I
had made up my mind coming home, and what you
said only strengthened it."

Dr. Markham looked at her in the utmost admiration. There were tears swimming upon her long
lashes, and every feature seemed to tremble with
the effort thus made; and Kathie appeared so sim-

ply lovely in her pure heroism, that the doctor stooped and kissed her forehead.

"My child," he said, tenderly, "you do not know how much your resolve pleases me. Your aunt is very fragile and delicate. She has been deprived of air and exercise, and doubtless overtasked her strength in the past days, so that now, when all the vital forces are needed, she has comparatively few at her command. Since we have talked of this second operation, I think she has taken a fancy that she was not doing as well as she ought, and it is of the utmost importance that she should be kept cheerful. She is very fond of you, and so if you can decide to remain —"

"I have already." Kathie's voice was low but steady.

"God will reward you, I am sure," said Mrs. Markham.

"Can I go up?" asked Kathie, timidly.

"Not just this moment, my dear; I hope she is asleep. And now you must try and encourage her, will you?"

"Yes," said Kathie, under her breath, though it sounded almost like a sob.

"Come to my room and take off your cloak," exclaimed Mrs. Markham. "My little darling, I don't wonder that they all love you, you are so sweet and generous."

"O Mrs. Markham, don't praise me too much! I felt at first as if I could n't. The Christmas at Cedarwood would be so very delightful if we could all be together. It seems as if it was the first real Christmas in my life."

"And this is why I honor you for the sacrifice, because I know it must have been hard."

Kathie leaned her head against the friendly bosom, and her tears fell silently, though they were not all tears of pain or disappointment.

CHAPTER X.

A FRESH TRIAL.

KATHIE could only go in and kiss Aunt Ruth that evening. Her face was as colorless as the pillow ; even her lips had lost their usual pale tint, and somehow her features looked sharp and sunken, and Kathie felt almost as if she were dying. When she was alone by herself in her little bed, she gave vent to the tears that had been so hard to repress.

It was a little strange, perhaps, but presently comfort came to her in the remembrance of some of the old talks she and Aunt Ruth had enjoyed together. It made her braver and more patient, and brought a firmer trust in God. It did not altogether seem as if *he* meant to send any great trouble upon them, like death, when they were all so happy. In this Kathie forgot her own disappointment.

The nurse remained in constant attendance on Sunday. Aunt Ruth was too weak for conversation, but Kathie glanced up now and then with a bright smile. Hard as it was, she determined to follow Dr. Markham's wishes as near as she could, and be cheerful even if she did not feel quite so buoyant at heart.

The event of Monday was Uncle Robert's visit, of course. He had been down twice, but only for a day or two, and this time he did not mean to hurry home. He was a good deal surprised at the turn affairs had taken, but, after an interview with Dr. Markham, felt satisfied that the wisest course had been followed.

Miss Jessie was delighted to see Kathie. She told her how all Brookside had missed her, and was laden with such a host of messages, from Charlie down to poor old Granny Thomas at the almshouse.

"I did n't suppose so many people would miss me," said Kathie, with a gay little smile. "It is very sweet to be remembered, — is n't it, Miss Jessie ? "

"Yes. And they 're all counting upon seeing you at Christmas. I think you will have to buy a regular Santa Claus stocking, no other will be large enough."

The bright look faded a little at this, but she did not mention her resolve, her heart felt so tender about it.

"It seems too unfortunate that your aunt will not be well enough to come, though I fancy your mamma scarcely expected it."

It was quite a relief to Kathie to hear that. Then Miss Jessie told her about being over at Cedarwood to tea, and how they had discussed the subject. Mrs. Alston was afraid it would be hardly prudent to take such a journey in midwinter, after having been so carefully housed.

Then they talked about Charlie, and how he was getting on at school, and he thought Rob was improving wonderfully and was going to make a real fine scholar. All the girls came in for a share, though some of them had written to Kathie, yet it was pleasant to hear the news over again.

Miss Jessie declined Mrs. Markham's invitation to stay to supper, so Uncle Robert attended her, to her uncle's.

"I shall come back and spend the evening with you," he whispered. "I've hardly had a glimpse of my little girl."

Kathie was not able to eat her supper for very gladness. She counted the moments until Uncle Robert's return.

They had the library all to themselves, — a small but cosey room containing some luxurious arm-chairs. In one of these Uncle Robert seated himself and took Kathie upon his knee.

"This is quite like old times," he declared. "I have missed you very much, Kathie."

"How dearly everybody must love me!" she said, simply. "I am glad that you all want me back."

"We could n't keep house without you"; and he laughed.

She asked him about the boys, and Freddy's pets, that were flourishing finely. It was good to hear so promising an account of Rob. And all the Morrisons were well and happy, and wanted to be remembered to Miss Kathie.

"I feel so sorry and disappointed about Aunt Ruth," Uncle Robert said, presently, "though your mamma was quite sure she would not be able to endure the journey. She appeared to be improving the last time I was here, and I had counted so strongly upon a merry Christmas party. Then it will be too bad to leave her here alone."

"She is not going to stay here alone," replied Kathie, in a low, grave tone.

"Not alone?   Why, Kathie, —"

"I am going to stay with her"; and Kathie put her head down on Uncle Robert's breast.

"Not come home for Christmas!" echoed Uncle Robert, in surprise.

"No"; and then Kathie told him all her story, her own half-formed resolves and her conversation with Dr. Markham.   Very truthfully and simply too, touching upon the disappointment which she still felt with all a child's keenness.

"My dear, noble girl, I have not a word to say. Of course Aunt Ruth would very willingly spare you, and the holidays at home will lose half their enjoyment.   But under the circumstances it is best to stay right on, and Aunt Ruth needs the comfort.   Poor child! it has been harder than any of us imagined in the beginning."

And then the tender lips kissed Kathie many times.   A brave, unselfish child indeed!

"We shall have to keep the Christmas until you do come home, even if it is out of date.   But I have promised the boys a tree and wax lights innumerable."

"I wish you would invite some of the children in

to see it. And I'd like to fly through the ceiling for five minutes and hear all the exclamations. How Freddy will enjoy it!"

"And Mr. Meredith is coming. He was up on Saturday and returned with us."

"Did he tell you about General Mackenzie? I liked him so much. He made me think of you continually, only he is a great deal older. And I wrote you that I went to an opera?"

"Yes. I am glad that you have had such a pleasant time."

"And I have n't been scarcely a bit homesick. Only now and then when I think of you all, and go to bed without a host of fond good-nights, it seems lonesome. Only if Aunt Ruth can live —"

"My darling, I hope she will. I pray for it hourly. Yet she does not look nearly so well as a fortnight ago, though that may be owing to her recent operation. We have no one to lose, — have we, Kathie?"

"Not one."

He held her tightly to his heart. Of all the duties he had taken upon himself since his return, the pleasantest was being a father to this fatherless little girl.

"And how does the purse hold out?" he asked, gayly.

"I am growing extravagant, I'm afraid. There are so many lovely things in the shop windows, and books that I want to read — "

"I shall have to examine your collection. I dare say it is sufficient to stock my Christmas-tree."

She laughed at this, though she had quite a formidable pile in one of the large bureau drawers. Some of them should go to Rob and Freddy.

At last Uncle Robert was forced to say good night. It was so like old times that Kathie clung to him and could hardly bear to unclasp her arms. But then there was to be a to-morrow.

A very gay, happy time they had, to be sure. For a week the nurse was with Aunt Ruth constantly, and the room was kept dark and quiet, so Kathie found herself at liberty to follow her own devices. The weather, which had been quite mild, turned very cold, and everybody was seized with a skating fit. Miss Jessie and she had kept up a constant visiting, but now they went to Central Park, their party increased by Mr. Meredith and Miss Ada.

Ada was wonderfully elegant. She wore the

prettiest, daintiest skating costume that could be imagined, and she was quite a proficient in the art. Kathie could do nothing but look on, for she had only tried two or three times with the other girls' skates at school, and had not made out very much. Ada glided hither and thither, followed by a host of admiring eyes.

"O, I wish I could skate!" exclaimed Kathie, longingly.

"My dear little girl, you shall have a chance to learn, at least. We will run up to-morrow morning and take our first lesson," answered Uncle Robert.

Mr. Meredith was on the ice awhile, but presently he left Ada to some of her boyish gallants, and rejoined the party standing on the bridge, telling Miss Jessie that it was a great oversight in not bringing her skates, and that he had half a mind to borrow a pair.

"Not to-day," she returned, smilingly. "But what a lovely skater your little niece is!"

"She is up in all the accomplishments," he returned, dryly. Then he patted Kathie's rosy cheek and commiserated her a little.

"She is going to try to-morrow morning," Uncle

12

Robert exclaimed. "I must invest in two pairs of skates to-night, though I don't know as I shall be able to stand up on them. Skating is wellnigh a lost art with me."

"And I'll bring Miss Jessie," said Mr. Meredith. "We will have a nice quiet time to ourselves before the crowd begins."

That evening they all went to a concert. The Meredith family carriage took them and brought them back, and Ada fancied that she made quite an impression.

But the morning Ada knew nothing about. They had a very comical time, though it must be confessed that Kathie did very well and distinguished herself by not more than half a dozen tumbles. Uncle Robert was rather awkward, but Miss Jessie skated beautifully, and they all enjoyed it very much.

A few days afterward Kathie went to tea at Ada's. The play in the nursery with the children was very delightful indeed, and Kathie told them some laughable little stories. They coaxed her into taking supper with them, and had Ada's beautiful china set. Kathie poured the tea, which they all thought a great treat.

" How very childish you are ! " Ada said, with dignity. " Why, I gave up playing with them long ago. They never expect it of me."

" They 're so sweet that I can't help loving them," returned Kathie, deprecatingly.

" And a great bore ! "

Kathie was silent. There were some subjects on while she and Ada did not agree.

" Is Miss Darrell going home when your uncle does ? " Ada asked, presently.

" Yes." She almost said, " And Mr. Meredith is going with them," but checked herself from some inward impulse.

" I suppose she is engaged to your uncle."

" Engaged ! " Kathie repeated, in completest surprise.

" Yes, engaged ! What a little innocent you are, Kathie Alston ! Why, I should have guessed it a long time ago if I had seen them together. And then his bringing her to the city, — lovers always do such things, you know. Besides, I think he is very devoted."

Kathie was struck dumb momentarily. Only it really did seem to her that of the two Mr. Meredith had shown the most devotion. He had been very solicitous for Miss Jessie's comfort, wrapping her well from the cold, and afraid she would fatigue herself skating too long, while Uncle Robert treated her like a friend or sister. Her brain seemed to be in a great maze of confusion.

"Then you don't like it?" said Ada, who had been watching the thoughtful face.

"Why, I like Miss Jessie very much; and if it were true, — yes, I think it would be real nice."

"Well, it *is* true; no one could have a doubt about it," returned Ada, in a very positive manner; "mamma was speaking of it —"

"Why, how did she know?" interrupted Kathie, with fresh amaze.

"Uncle Edward has mentioned Miss Darrell several times, and you know we all went to the concert. She is very pretty and pleasant, but mamma thinks it would be a rather unfortunate thing for you all."

Ada had been present at a trifling conversation between her parents on the subject, and she was making the most of her knowledge.

"Why, she would be our aunt, you know," said Kathie, with pleasant frankness.

"But she would come to live at Cedarwood, and be mistress."

"There's plenty of room, I am sure."

"O, what a goose you are, Kathie! She might not want your mother nor your Aunt Ruth there, and she might not like to have *her* husband spend so much money on you all. You know you would n't have any real claim then, neither would it be *your* house."

"I don't believe Miss Jessie would feel so at all," said Kathie, indignantly.

"But your mother would have a good deal of delicacy about it, and I should think it would be real hard to be poor again. Then, you know, he could n't leave his fortune to you, and he would be very likely to have children of his own."

Poor Kathie! Her vision of pleasant years gloomed over, though she could n't believe marrying Miss Jessie would make such a difference.

"It is too bad, Kathie," Ada went on, sympathizingly; "I should not even like Uncle Edward to marry, for he gives me so many pretty things, and takes me out, and when I am a young lady it will be so nice to have him, for he is a good deal younger than papa, and handsomer too; so I should feel awfully cross.

"I don't feel cross," said Kathie; but her lip quivered and the tears almost came in her eyes. "We should try to be happy; and we do love Miss Jessie very much. I don't believe it would be — quite so bad."

"If you had an income of your own; but to be dependent upon your uncle for every penny, and to feel that his wife considered you a burden — "

"We will not talk any more about it," said Kathie, suddenly, for her heart was almost breaking.

Ada had felt a little sore over General Mackenzie's preference, and she rather enjoyed the idea of being even with Kathie, as she would have termed it; and she said to herself that it was all true, she had advanced no opinions but those she had heard her mother utter. Whether it was kind or necessary she never considered, for she was not much used to studying the happiness of other people.

Then they went down to the piano, and Ada played while they both sang. At first Kathie thought she could not steady her voice; but the effort took her mind from the mountain of apprehension that loomed up before her.

The two girls sang very beautifully together. Kathie had a fine, clear soprano voice, while Ada's was a very rich alto, every one said, for a child. Mrs. Meredith was exceedingly proud of her daughter, and liked to have her admired, while Ada was nowise loath to be brought forward.

Two or three friends dropped in presently and were much entertained. Kathie hoped that Mr. Edward Meredith would make his appearance, but he did not. What would both girls have said if they had known that he was spending the evening with Miss Jessie, at her uncle's, and being " most devoted " ?

On the whole, Kathie was rather glad to go home. They sent her in the carriage with the nursery-maid, a very nice, pleasant girl, who thought Kathie the sweetest being that she had ever seen. Uncle Robert had been passing most of the evening with Aunt Ruth, who had begun to rally a little, and he was finishing by a talk with Mrs. Markham.

" Well, Pussy," he exclaimed, kissing her fondly, " did you have a nice time ? "

She clung to him with strange tenderness. O, could she ever bear to give him up to another, even if that other was Miss Jessie ?

"It was very pleasant," she answered, in a quiet tone, and then she sat on his knee until he was ready to go.

"Only two days more," he said at the hall door. "I shall be very sorry not to take you with me, little one, yet I am glad to have you stay with Aunt Ruth. I feel quite sure that she will get well. To-morrow you must go out and buy some Christmas with me."

She went up to kiss Aunt Ruth good night.

"My darling," the invalid said, "Uncle Robert has told me of your resolve to stay. It is so kind and generous in you, but I do not feel quite as if I could allow such a sacrifice."

"It really will not be hard for me, Aunt Ruth," she answered, sweetly. "And if I were home I should be thinking of you and how lonesome you were, and it would make the Christmas less merry. You have done so many kind things for all of us children, especially me, that I ought to make some return."

"But this is a great deal, Kathie. And I think I would rather have you go home for a week or two, even if you came back. It may be two months before I can venture to travel."

"I believe I would rather stay right along," Kathie

answered, quietly. "I ought to do this, Aunt Ruth, and I ought to be learning to endure some of the — trials of life," and she hesitated a little. "Uncle Robert said he was glad that I had resolved to stay. And then mamma thinks of coming as soon as she can be spared."

"You are a dear little girl, and I hope God will reward you by a happy future."

But while Kathie was saying her prayers the slow tears would fill her eyes in spite of her efforts at calmness. Somehow there was a lonely foreboding that she could not quite overcome. What if all their lives should be changed presently as Ada had suggested! And then her heart filled with thankfulness at the prospect of Aunt Ruth's recovery.

They had a pleasant time buying Christmas gifts, but Kathie was much graver than usual. Uncle Robert attributed it to a lingering disappointment at not being able to return home as she had wished, and was not surprised at it. He was very tender and considerate, and it seemed more than once as if she must tell him what was on her mind.

"It would be selfish not to care for his happiness as well," she thought to herself, and was silent.

The parting came hard, after all, though Uncle
Robert was merry to the last moment. Mr. Meredith
ran in too, to say good by.

"I 'll appropriate your share of the Christmas-
tree," he announced, gayly. "If I should make myself sick eating dainties, it will be in a good cause,
you know."

Then he kissed her and did what was very odd,
she thought, — linked Miss Jessie's hand in his arm
and marched her out of the waiting-room to the
car. She was talking and smiling, and looked bright
and happy as a queen.

Dr. Markham lifted Kathie in his buggy and
tucked the wolf robe around her, for he had brought
her down to see the travellers off. Studying her a
moment, he said, in a tone of great tenderness,
"That's a brave little face. My child, you are learning some of the best lessons of life."

Kathie's chin quivered, and a tear dropped on the robe.

"When you are a woman and have severer trials,
as nearly all men and women do, you will look back
at this and be thankful for the strength and courage
gained now. I am so glad for your aunt's sake."

With that commendation Kathie was content.

CHAPTER XI.

KATHIE'S CHRISTMAS.

IT seemed to Kathie that she had never known anything so quiet as the two days that followed. On Saturday there was no music, as Mrs. Gifford had gone away on a visit, and on Sunday it snowed. She sat in Aunt Ruth's room sewing or reading, and not saying much, for the invalid was not sufficiently strong for conversations of any length. Kathie made an admirable attendant in a sick-room on account of her rare gift of tender silence. Now and then she glanced up with a smile, she moved a pillow or brought a drink, and made no confusion. She never stumbled against any article of furniture, or dropped anything she took in her hand. Part of this ease came by nature, but much of it from her habit of studying the comfort of others. She tried to *think*, and though that is not always easy to do, it brings an exceeding great reward.

Aunt Ruth could not sit up at all now, though all

her symptoms were favorable, except that her appetite was so very slender.   Indeed, this had been a
difficulty all along, and added to the anxieties of the
case.   Kathie could do better with her than the
nurse, and this was one reason why Dr. Markham
had not wished to spare her, even for a few days, at
this crisis.

Kathie felt really glad that it was not necessary
to make an effort at conversation.   She had much to
think of during these days.   Visions of home that
were most tempting floated in upon her, and a longing for mamma that made her heart ache ; for giving
up the visit had not been an easy thing.

The entire change, too, made it appear more lonesome.   No Uncle Robert dropping in for a pleasant
call, and no events of any kind to break the monot-
ony.   Even Dr. Markham seemed unusually busy,
and she scarcely saw him.   The weather was not
very fine, for on Monday it snowed again.

But Christmas morning dawned beautifully ; Kathie
heard the bells ringing in the clear air, and her heart
went up in praise and thanksgiving.   Unconsciously
she said to herself part of a hymn that she had
learned the year before and almost forgotten : —

" Wake me, that I the twelvemonth long
   May bear the song
About with me in the world's throng ;
That treasured joys of Christmas-tide
May with mine hour of gloom abide ;
   The Christmas carol ring
Deep in my heart, when I would sing ;
   Each of the twelve good days
Its earnest yield of duteous love and praise,
Insuring happy months and hallowing common ways."

And then a stray glimpse of that time swept over her brain, — the little kitchen with its rag-carpet, and three stockings hanging just below the mantel. How gay they had all been, laughing and talking and wishing merry Christmases, the voices growing louder and louder until mamma had to check them. And how many lovely things had happened all through the year ! Yes, she must be glad and thankful, and bear about with her the many treasured joys that God had given. Had she really been repining in thought for the last few days ? Well, she would remember the happy home faces, but not long for anything that she missed. It would all come back in good time.

The brightest and sweetest face in the world bent

over and kissed Aunt Ruth's pale lips, and the tender voice murmured its fond greeting.

"My dear child, how happy you look!" was Aunt Ruth's surprised exclamation.

"I am happy," was the joyous reply.

"I have been thinking of you ever since I woke, and, O Kathie, it seemed so hard to keep you here when you might be enjoying so much more pleasure. If it was n't the first Christmas at Cedarwood — and there may never be another that could have been so happy." Aunt Ruth's eyes filled with tears.

There was a great throb in Kathie's heart, and she tried to steady the quiver in her voice.

"Dear Aunt Ruth," she said, "it is all right and best as it is. Why should n't I give up a little pleasure for you ? If I were ill you would do it willingly. Dr. Markham approves of my staying, and so did Uncle Robert, and now you shall see how merry I am going to be. First I shall bathe your face and hands, and then see about your breakfast. It is a glorious day ! Look at the sun."

Aunt Ruth was soon made ready. Kathie ran down to the kitchen and begged the nurse to let her toast some bread. Her mother had a fashion of making very delightful milk toast, and Kathie did this to a charm. Then there was a rare bit out of the tenderloin steak to broil.

"I did everything myself," she exclaimed, laughingly. "Cook is going to give me a recommendation when I want a new place!"

"The odor is quite tempting," was Aunt Ruth's reply.

"And you must eat it all."

They had quite a gay time over the breakfast, and for a wonder Aunt Ruth's appetite appeared improved.

"I believe I really do feel better," she exclaimed, much encouraged.

"Good tidings," said Kathie, "and it will be a great joy to me!"

"Now you must run down to the dining-room yourself, for there goes the bell."

"I think I'll take the Afghan with me"; and Kathie brought it out of the closet. "It is not quite finished, but I can do that afterward; and to-day seems the time for gifts."

She had spent all her leisure time upon it, and it

was very pretty indeed. Crocheted in stripes, the alternate ones being black, embroidered with bright flowers. A little of the work still remained to be done, for Kathie had met with so many interruptions during the past fortnight. She wrapped herself in it, laughing gayly, and stole softly down.

Dr. Markham was just coming out of his office. "Who is this?" he exclaimed, catching her in his arms, for she was enveloped head and ears.

"Santa Claus," she made answer, in a rather smothered tone of voice.

"What has he sent me, you little rogue of a messenger? Three good kisses, three good wishes — "

"'And a slice of ginger' done up in this," she answered, with which the Afghan fell at his feet.

"This is the ginger, then, I suppose?" and he kissed her rosy cheek. "But, seriously, Miss Kathie, all this gay — Why, it's a carriage-blanket! and I doubt if it came down the chimney, it looks so fresh and beautiful."

Mrs. Markham ventured out of the breakfast-room. She had been in the secret, and enjoyed the surprised look of the doctor very much.

"I think these little fingers had something to do with it," she said, clasping Kathie's hand.

"My dear child, — for me? Why, you are the dearest little Santa Claus I ever saw! I don't know what to say to you. I have half a mind to steal you from your kith and kin and take you to the moon, wrapped in this blanket."

"Let her have a little breakfast first, for I don't believe they have muffins and chocolate in the moon," interposed Mrs. Markham.

"I must tell you that you have an invitation to a Christmas-tree to-night at my nephew's. I wish there was a branch of it round here just now"; and the doctor's eyes twinkled.

Kathie turned her plate over after she was seated. A small, square, red Russia-leather box lay underneath. There was a tiny, golden ornamented scroll, containing her own name, set in the top.

"A miniature!" she exclaimed.

"Open it"; and the doctor smiled.

There was a card on which was written, "To my darling Kathie. R. C."

"Uncle Robert. Oh!" And then for a moment Kathie could do nothing but look. The loveliest watch imaginable, the case richly engraved, and bits of enamelled leaves that seemed set with

13

diamonds, while attached was a very handsome chain.

"You knew about this," Kathie said, glancing up at the doctor, with a bright smile.

"Yes, it was left in my charge."

Kathie's face was one glow of delight, good to behold. She could hardly eat her breakfast, so full of pleasure was every nerve and every breath.

"I must go up stairs with you," the doctor said, "or I am afraid you will set Miss Conover wild; and I can't have my patient tampered with."

So they went together, Kathie hopping up two steps at a time; but the doctor held her hand tightly, and would not let her get much in advance.

"Your business comes afterward, being of less importance," he began, gravely nodding his head to Kathie, as he helped himself to a chair and greeted his patient cordially.

"Why, here is quite a pulse instead of the mere thread I 've had to hunt for the last fourteen days," he said, in surprise. "Have you been getting up an excitement?"

"I really do feel better," Aunt Ruth returned. "I ate quite a breakfast."

"O, you 'll be frisking about with the best of them next year this time, hanging up your stocking and all that nonsense! I dare say we shall have you dancing a jig."

Kathie laughed at this, it seemed so very amusing.

"Yes, there is a decided improvement. I think you are well enough to hear about my Christmas!"

He told the most comical story imaginable, in which Kathie scarcely recognized herself, but his hearer enjoyed it immensely.

Here there was an interruption. Mrs. Havens, Kathie's old friend, who had been away on a visit and but just returned, sent to know if Kathie would not like to go to church with her. The children were to sing some beautiful carols.

Kathie looked undecided, and raised her eyes to Aunt Ruth.

"Of course you will," said the doctor. "You want a sniff of fresh air, and by that time your auntie will desire a quiet rest. Go and keep Christmas — I need not add with a happy heart, for you always have that."

Then he gave a few directions to Miss Conover and left them together. Kathie displayed her beautiful gift.

"'T is just what I have been wishing for, Aunt Ruth, but Uncle Robert was always doing so many kind things that it seemed ungrateful to ask for any other gift. O my little darling, you 're just good enough to kiss for dear Uncle Robert's sake."

" It is very lovely, and I am so glad to see you enjoy it thoroughly."

" And, Aunt Ruth, you think — you feel sure that Uncle Robert will always love us ? "

She knelt down by the bed and buried her face close to Aunt Ruth's cheek. It seemed treason to doubt any one so kind. Somehow she wished Ada had not mentioned the surmise.

"My darling, yes. God has sent us one of the dearest and kindest of friends. While he lives, we shall not lack for tender care."

Yes, it was selfish and wicked to grudge him any happiness, and if he wanted to marry Miss Jessie they would all rejoice over it. Not another troubled thought could she admit. He would always love them, and that was sufficient. With that Kathie's burden fell away, and it was just as if she entered in at the gate Beautiful.

She thought so as she sat in church with Mrs. Havens listening to the joyous carols. A throng of happy children raising their sweet young voices in glorious hymns of rejoicing, and the great organ tones swelling out strains that were inspiration. Kathie's heart was full, moved to the uttermost. It seemed to her that there was not room for another throb of satisfaction.

Mrs. Havens would fain have taken Kathie home with her, but the child could not leave Aunt Ruth so long on this of all days. She found her comfortable and in cheerful spirits, and it did seem as if she were really getting well.

Several medical friends of the doctor were in to dinner, and Kathie saw no more of him until eight in the evening, though she had been happy enough. Then he called her down and tucked her in the sleigh beside Mrs. Markham, and they drove off to Mr. Meredith's.

The lights in the drawing-room were so bright that it looked as if they might be having a party. And a party sure enough it proved. The room was quite

full, some of the neighbors having been invited in,
as well as the relatives, and one whom she hardly
expected to see, — Mr. Edward Meredith.

He clasped both hands and wished her merry
Christmas a dozen times. The evening before he
had been at Cedarwood.

"They missed you very much, you may be sure";
he said. "Those little Gardiner girls were over, and
one or two others, — and Charlie Darrell — "

"And Miss Jessie, of course ? "

"Yes." At that Mr. Meredith looked rather
peculiar, and a warm flush suffused Kathie's face.
He had guessed the truth as well as Ada.

"Tell me about the tree. What did Freddy have,
and how did he enjoy it ? "

"O, the child went nearly crazy. It was a complete surprise to him, for he had no idea how a
Christmas-tree looked. But he wanted to hang up
his stocking all the same."

That made Kathie laugh.

"Uncle Edward," said Ada, "here are the children
clamoring for Kathie. She has spoiled them by so
much attention, and they can't understand that a
drawing-room is n't a nursery. Kathie, how do you
do ? Have you had any Christmas yet ? "

"This"; and Kathie displayed her watch.

"O, how lovely! Why, it's handsomer than mine."

"Want to see!" said Florence, pushing her curly head between the two dresses.

"You have n't kissed me," exclaimed George. "A good, sweet Christmas kiss!"

"And me!" said Master Willie, eagerly.

"What a nuisance!" and Ada gave her head a toss. "Don't let them have your watch, Kathie; they'll break it to fragments."

She held it for them to admire. They climbed over her and kissed her to their hearts' content.

"And we're going to have a real Santa Claus!" announced George.

"Will he come down the chimney?" was Kathie's merry question as she looked at them with laughing eyes.

"He'd get a little burned," said Florence, with a wise shake of the head.

"A good deal, I guess, and all black. Do Santa Clauses come down the chimney Kathie?" asked Willie, rather perplexed.

"So people say!"

"Did you ever see him?"

"O, I used to hang up my stocking and go to bed."

"Children!" exclaimed their mother. "Mary, don't let them annoy Miss Kathie."

"Here is a Santa Claus," said Ada, looking back from a group of very fashionably attired little girls.

The children held their breath and opened their eager eyes. Mary raised Florence in her arms.

The folding doors between the drawing-room and library opened slowly. There was the tree, its widespread arms glittering with burning tapers and tiny brilliantly colored balls that swung tremulously in the heated air. After they had partly taken in this, the younger ones uttered an exclamation of surprise and delight, for there was a veritable Santa Claus.

A comical personage, enormously stout, and wrapped in furs from head to foot, with a fur cap upon his head. His cheeks were puffy and red as the reddest apple, his nose was a little hooked one way, and his pointed chin turned up so that the two nearly met. He had the broadest grin on his countenance, and

KATHIE'S CHRISTMAS.   Page 199.

altogether he was a funny-looking object, to say noth-ing of the great pack slung upon his back.

The children gave a shout of glee. Willie wanted to run and speak to him, and thought Mary very cruel because she restrained him.

Santa Claus rang a little bell, and began to make a speech. He was travelling around, he said, to find good children. He had some gifts in his bag for them, but all those who had been naughty during the year had better go to bed, he thought.

"I 've been good," said Willie, boldly.

"And I 've been good," echoed Florence.

George laughed, but said nothing. Several of the little ones around looked quite sober.

Santa Claus put down his pack.

He worked and tugged at the straps, puffing and blowing, and they came apart at length with such an impetus that he almost sprawled on the floor, at which nearly every one laughed. Then he fumbled about, and at last drew forth a package. Here he had to stop and search his pockets for an enormous pair of green spectacles before he could read the name.

George was first. He went up boldly, and bore off his gift in triumph. Then Willie was summoned who advanced rather cautiously. Two or three others, then Kathie Alston's name was called. She colored rather vividly, and went up with some shyness.

"Open it," said George, "I'll let you see mine."

There were half a dozen papers at least, then a dainty velvet case. Inside a brooch, ear-rings, and sleeve-buttons of white onyx, very handsomely set. Two initials were on a card, — "A. M." She glanced up at Mrs. Markham with a grateful smile. Ada came to inspect.

"They are very pretty," she said, "only there are so many imitations of onyx."

That did not spoil the pleasure for Kathie, however.

There were a great many funny things in that wonderful pack of Santa Claus. The children laughed, and so did the grown people. Dogs that would bark, cats that would mew, a comical little man who always would turn a somersault before he could settle himself, and numberless oddities. And when he could find no more he turned it inside out and shook it, and then he came to the tree.

There were numerous gifts for the elders here. Kathie was more than surprised to find herself remembered by so many friends. Mrs. Havens had sent a beautiful glove-box containing half a dozen pairs of gloves in different colors; Mrs. Meredith, some pretty handkerchiefs with her initials embroidered in the corner; from Mr. Edward Meredith a necklace and cross; from Dr. Markham a set of books bound very handsomely, and, best of all, a dear remembrance from mamma, that had come from the Christmas-tree at Cedarwood.

"Where is your uncle?" asked Kathie of Ada presently. In the excitement and confusion she had but just missed him.

Ada laughed and looked mysterious.

"Oh!" said Kathie, and then she smiled at the Santa Claus, who was making a final speech and bowing himself away.

How odd that she had not suspected it, for it did not seem to her that any one else could have been quite as amusing.

Then all the children thronged round the tree. The candies were crunched, the fruit divided, everybody laughed and talked, and declared that it had been most delightful. Kathie could only clasp the hands that were so fondly extended to her, and smile her thanks, for her heart was full.

The younger children were dismissed to the nursery, as it was long past their bedtime. A few of the smaller visitors went home, and the rest had quite an amusing hour to themselves. Kathie was perfectly radiant with happiness.

"The prettiest child here," said Dr. Markham, with pardonable pride, "and the best behaved. She acts like a little girl, not a fine lady, who must turn up her nose at everything. George's daughter is being spoiled as fast as possible. I wonder if her mother thinks such airs and affectations becoming? Kathie will make a lovely woman, but Ada will be simply insufferable!"

There was more than one who admired Kathie. Ada was fairly jealous of the attention bestowed upon her.

But Dr. Markham declared at last that they were steady old people, and not much used to dissipation, so they must travel off home. Kathie was quite bewildered with the hosts of kisses and fond good-bys.

"I have ever so much more to tell you, so I shall come round," said Mr. Meredith to Kathie as they stood in the hall.

"I shall shut Kathie in a band-box," growled Dr. Markham. "I will not have the young men running after her!"

"He is very cruel!" said Uncle Edward, with a comical sigh. "If he bolts the doors I shall drop down the chimney."

"The loveliest time in the world," whispered Kathie surreptitiously to Aunt Ruth. "It will take you all day to-morrow to look at my presents. I don't believe I could have been any happier at Cedarwood, and I wonder why everybody is so kind and sweet to me. To be loved is the very best thing of all, dear Aunt Ruth."

CHAPTER XII.

CRUMBS OF COMFORT.

AUNT RUTH really had begun to improve, there could be no mistake in the fact. Her appetite was better, her spirits more buoyant, and she was gaining strength ; indeed, she seemed much more like her olden self, hopeful and smiling. Dr. Markham was very much encouraged, and Kathie was brimful of delight.

She had written home a very glowing account of her Christmas, and she felt so grateful for the two remembrances from those she loved best, mamma and Uncle Robert. She held her watch quite in awe, and was almost afraid to wind it, or even to wear it.

On the first day of the new year Dr. Markham allowed Aunt Ruth to try sitting up again in the re-clining-chair. It did not tire her as much as before.

"I expect that we shall soon hear of your running away," he exclaimed, laughingly.

Kathie came and sat by her, and held her hand in tender, wistful love.

"I feel like giving thanks every moment," she said. "It's so delightful to think of your getting well."

"Yes, my darling"; and a thoughtful shade crossed Aunt Ruth's face.

"I was almost afraid —" began Kathie; but she stopped in a little awe, for there is always something solemn in the thought of death.

Aunt Ruth's fingers tightened in their clasp.

"I have been near to the brink of the dark river," she said, slowly. "I was weak, and full of repinings."

"Why, Aunt Ruth!" exclaimed Kathie, in surprise. "We all thought you very patient. I never heard you utter a complaint. But it seems to me that it would be hard to die now, — when we are all so happy."

"And that was the lesson I had to learn. I believe I was not quite satisfied or resigned until the dawn of Christmas. When I gave up my will, God showed me his, which was better than my weak fears."

"But did you really think that you would die?"

"My dear child, I have had some dreary weeks

lying here. But for your tender care and bright,
hopeful face, it seemed sometimes as if my slender
hold on life must have ended. I can never tell you
all the comfort you have been to me."

Kathie guessed now why Dr. Markham had been
so anxious to have her stay. Perhaps he had considered Aunt Ruth in a critical condition.

" I don't know," she said, with a perplexed expression, "how any one can be *quite* satisfied to die. Does
God mean that we shall be glad to leave those we
love and everything sweet and dear?"

" He means us to be resigned to his will, and to
try to be happy in it. When we were very poor and
had few enjoyments he sent Uncle Robert to us. I
suppose if I had been very ill before that, I should
have felt quite satisfied to die, for I seemed only a
burden in my helplessness."

"O Aunt Ruth, it was so nice to have you then!"
interrupted Kathie, eagerly. "Yet I want you just
as much now and all the time."

The invalid smiled.

" Tell me what you thought of then, Kathie said,
presently.

" My darling, lying there in a hopeless mood, for I

seemed to lose every day, I felt that death was not only possible, but near. And it appeared hard to die just when we had come to comfort and happiness. Then the second operation discouraged me a good deal. I am afraid I grew quite rebellious. I dreaded to be left alone even for a few days, so you see I was selfish."

"But you did not speak of it. You were willing that I should go home."

"Yes, I made myself so. I put a curb upon my tongue and kept silent, like the Psalmist, even from good words, for I did not want to have you stay against your will. And then your generosity taught me a lesson. I committed my ways into the Lord, and resolved to trust in him, to take life or death and be content. During the intervals, when I could not sleep, I prayed for resignation; and though I can never tell quite how it was, as the morning dawned I felt satisfied that he would do what was best."

"And God answered all our prayers," Kathie said, with sweet seriousness. "I know mamma and Uncle Robert thought of it at home."

"So you see, my love, we have to learn lessons over constantly, for we never get them perfect."

14

Kathie was quiet and thoughtful for many moments, then she said, in a low tone, "Aunt Ruth, I have had a lesson to learn also."

"What was it?" with a sweet smile.

"Being generous."

"I fancied you made a great sacrifice in staying with me."

"O, it was n't that, Aunt Ruth"; and Kathie colored. "It did seem a little hard at first; but after Dr. Markham thought it would be better for me to remain, I became quite content about it. I could see that you really did need me; and when you had done so much for my pleasure and comfort, when you had even consented to be doctored because I wished it so very much, it was only right that I should stay."

"What was the trouble then?"

"It was not told to me as any secret," began Kathie, with a conscious blush, "but it *is* repeating a story, and mamma, you know, never liked to have me do it. Aunt Ruth, did you ever think that — Uncle Robert — would marry Miss Jessie Darrell?"

Aunt Ruth started in surprise. "Marry!" she

echoed, and Kathie saw that the idea was quite new new to her; "why, child, what put that into your head ?"

"Ada was talking about it. She said her mamma had been discussing it, and I suppose her Uncle Edward. He would be most likely to know."

"Tell me what she said, Kathie," was Aunt Ruth's grave question.

Kathie repeated the conversation very truthfully, though with some blushes and embarrassment.

"And this troubles you ?" A stray smile lurked about Aunt Ruth's face.

"O," exclaimed Kathie, imploringly, "do you think it would make such a difference ? Would we have to go away, and be poor again ?"

"Suppose we did, my darling ?"

"I should be very sorry to lose Uncle Robert, and to give up Cedarwood ; but the money is all his, and he has been so good already, — and if he would love us a little afterward — " Kathie's eyes filled with tears.

"My dear child, Ada is quite mistaken. There will be no change for us at present."

"But, Aunt Ruth — "

" Kathie, is n't there another view of the case ? "
and Aunt Ruth's smile deepened.

" That Miss Jessie could come to Cedarwood, and
love us, and that we might all live together —"

" Not quite that either."

Kathie looked bewildered.

" I am glad you are not as sharp in these matters
as Ada. When Uncle Robert was here he made
a guess or a surmise on better grounds, — that Miss
Jessie —"

" O Aunt Ruth, you don't mean that it is Mr
Meredith ? " exclaimed Kathie, as a light broke in
upon her mind.

" Ada's uncle instead of yours."

" But Ada will not like it ! "

" My dear Kathie, children's opinions on such
subjects are not of much importance. I think it
was very unkind in Ada to repeat anything like
that to you, even if it had been true. I dislike a
taste for gossip, especially if it is ill-natured, in
little girls, or in any one, in fact. So your trouble
is quite without foundation."

Kathie still looked serious.

" Do you not feel quite satisfied about it ? " asked
her aunt.

"I was thinking of Uncle Robert," returned Kathie, slowly. "I want him to be happy, and it almost seems as if I ought not feel *very* glad — "

"My dear child, set your mind at ease. What will happen when Uncle Robert marries we can hardly tell, but I think it will not be until you children are grown a little older and more capable of caring for yourselves. It is very kind of him to take charge of us all in this loving, generous manner, and yet, suppose he had come home without a penny and in poor health, what would your mamma have done?"

"O, we should all have been kind to him, Aunt Ruth, and worked for him. I would have done anything that I could."

"He knows this. Besides his generous heart, he has a great deal in his power, as people always have when they make a right use of money, and he is not one to begin a good work and then leave it before any result is accomplished. So we may enjoy our happiness without fear. But what conclusion had you reached?" and Aunt Ruth glanced encouragingly in the soft eyes.

"I was a good deal troubled at first"; and Kathie smiled a little at the bugbear, dwindling to a very

small shadow indeed.   "And then I guess I must
have followed your plan, — to look at the duties near
by, and leave those a long way off until I came to
them."

"Like the man who never crossed a bridge until
he reached it.   But why did you not tell me of this
before ? "

"Because you were so very poorly then, and Dr.
Markham forbade your being excited about anything," was Kathie's simple answer.

"You have been a brave and thoughtful girl, my
darling, and I hope you will have your reward."

Aunt Ruth kissed the fair forehead with deep
tenderness, and Kathie saw that there were tears in
her eyes.

"I don't want you to think that I was very miserable," she returned, smilingly.   "Christmas was a
happy time for me too, and it seems now as if God
had been watching, and sent me all the best joys and
gifts that any one could have.   Everything is coming
out just right."

Kathie looked so bright and satisfied that her face
was a perfect picture.

"And now one word before we leave the subject.

Do not mention this to Ada. If Mr. Meredith spoke of it to his sister-in-law, he may have some very good reason for evading publicity at present, and I should not like to have him trace any foolish stories to us."

Kathie promised, though her kind heart would have kept her from any such triumph as that which Ada had delighted to make known.

Mr. Edward Meredith had not taken part in the conversation, as Ada had led Kathie to understand. He had preserved a discreet silence whenever Miss Darrell's name was mentioned, though Mrs. Meredith had taken up the subject quite eagerly, and not been at all backward in giving her opinions.

Kathie could not help feeling light-hearted. It seemed as if all her troubles had suddenly come to an end, and the path was brightest sunshine. Two months would soon pass, and then for dear, delightful home and the boys.

But when Kathie went to her music that afternoon, her fingers were as full as her brain, and took unwarrantable liberties.

" You are falling back into some of the old habits," Mrs. Gifford said, by way of a check.

"People have to think every moment of the time if they want to do right," — and an odd little smile crossed Kathie's face ; "but it is very hard when one is real happy."

"Then you fancy that trouble and sorrow make one thoughtful ?"

"Yes, it is good to have had a little trouble," said Kathie, meditatively ; and she went on with the soberest of fingering. She was doing very well indeed, though it seemed slow work to her.

The second week in January Mrs. Alston came to the city. She had not mentioned any particular day, and Kathie had gone to have a little romp with the Meredith children. Florence wanted her to tend her beautiful Christmas doll, that was already growing rather the worse for wear ; but as it could open its eyes, and make an odd little sound, when you pressed it, that the children declared was saying, "Mamma," the child could hardly bear to have it out of her arms. Willie wanted to hear about the wonderful cat and little Red Riding-Hood ; and she must tell George about the rabbits and guinea-pigs that Freddy had in the barn ; and altogether it was quite late when she ran off home. In the dusk, she thought the lady sitting by the grate was Mrs. Markham.

"Kathie!" said a soft voice.

"O mamma, mamma!" and the next instant she was in her mother's arms, actually crying for joy.

Two months since she had kissed the dear lips or been held to the warm heart; and no one can ever be quite like a mother, as Kathie well knew.

"But if I had imagined you were here I should have come direct from Mrs. Gifford's," was her announcement.

"Then I suppose Aunt Ruth finds Ada quite a rival?" her mamma asked.

"O, this visit was to the children; I have to call on Ada separate days. She does n't like the nursery very much, and I do."

Then Kathie was not getting spoiled by the companionship.

Mrs. Alston was delighted to find Aunt Ruth so much improved, and with such a fair prospect of recovery; but her joy was fully as complete and satisfactory in her little daughter. It had been quite an ordeal for Kathie. Most of the time Aunt Ruth had been too ill to take any charge of her, or correct bad habits in their formation. That Kathie would be indulged and flattered Mrs. Alston well knew ; but she had hardly been prepared for the self-denial and strength that Aunt Ruth recounted of her.

Kathie wanted to hear everything, just as if there had never been a letter from Cedarwood, and she had to rehearse all the holiday doings and display her numerous gifts. It was such a delight to catch mamma's smiles, and to hear the dear, familiar tones, though now and then some word brought the tears to Kathie's eyes, to be laughed away the next moment. They were wonderfully happy, those three people.

CHAPTER XIII.

TAKING UP THE CROSS.

For a week Kathie was filled with supremest content. The music practices were given up, and even the two lessons were something of a trial. It seemed to her that she had hardly known the pleasure of having a mother; indeed, she had not been as dear after her sojourn in the city as now. For during Kathie's period of housekeeping Uncle Robert had been her friend and adviser nearly all the time, but here she had been compelled to depend a great deal upon herself.

It had not injured her in any respect. She was the same glad, happy, unaffected child, or if she had changed it was only to grow more considerate.

"And you think you can stay contentedly until Aunt Ruth is able to be moved?" her mother asked.

"O yes," said Kathie. "Though I wonder when it will be?"

"Some time in March, the doctor says."

"Mamma, I wish you were not going back so soon. Maybe it will be two months."

"In all probability as long as that. I shall come down again at the last, but it is quite difficult to be spared from home. The boys always seem to go wrong."

"Did you think they were very — bad, when you went home?" asked Kathie, hesitatingly.

"Rob had improved, I fancied, but Freddy gets astray rather easily; then you were there to look after them a little, you know, and now Uncle Robert has the whole charge. I don't like to put so much upon him very often."

Kathie could see that it was right for her mother to go, and yet there was a faintness about her heart whenever she thought of the separation.

"Is Rob doing well in his studies?"

"Quite nicely, I believe. But he is getting to be a large boy, and fancies himself of a great deal of importance. I believe I'd like to keep you all little for a good many years to come."

"O mamma, I hope we shall be a comfort, instead of a trouble, as we grow larger."

"My dear child, I feel certain that you will."

"But Rob is as good as most boys, mamma, except Charlie Darrell."

"And I suppose it is folly to wish him like any other boy, since he must be himself"; and Mrs. Alston smiled. "Mothers are always anxious. When one hears of bad men one trembles for the boys."

"Mamma," said Kathie, with a sort of dainty shyness, "Aunt Ruth·and I have given up· carrying burdens."

"And I ought, — is that what you think?"

Kathie blushed rosy red.

Mrs. Alston stooped to kiss her. "My darling," she said, "you have learned one very important lesson. It is folly to be so anxious about a future that is in God's hands. If we could be sure that we were doing our best, — but when we look back, we see where we might have been wiser."

This was beyond the reach of Kathie's reasoning, so she could only press mamma's hand and resolve that she would cause her as little pain as possible. And she breathed a fervent prayer that Rob might grow better every day.

But Kathie woke one morning with a heavy heart.

There was no storm, not a single cloud in the sky, so mamma must go home. Aunt Ruth felt very sorry also. Kathie's heart kept swelling up to her throat, and it seemed as if every mouthful of breakfast would choke her. Dr. Markham was to take them to the station, and he was a little brusque and disposed to tease, as was very apt to be his way when those around him were on the verge of sentiment. Mrs. Alston and he had discussed Aunt Ruth's case, and now there appeared no probability of further trouble ; indeed, she had nothing to do but get well as fast as circumstances would admit.

"Still, it has been quite a critical case," said the doctor. "She had much less strength than I thought for in the beginning, and at one time she quite lost heart. I find now that Kathie was the best ally we could have had. A grown person, more conscious of the danger, might have given way to discouraging forebodings ; but the child's faith was something exquisite. Because she wanted her to recover she would think of nothing against it, and her bright, happy temperament has been like sunshine, for all she is more thoughtful than most girls of her age. You hardly know what a treasure you have !"

It made Mrs. Alston very happy to hear Kathie so warmly praised. She had considered it quite a risk to allow Kathie to remain so long away from home without a mother's watchful eye, and exposed to much flattery and indulgence. She was very thankful that her child had passed the ordeal so well, and that some of the lessons of her past childhood were bearing fruit, so she left her now with a more satisfied heart.

The sisters bade each other good by hopefully. Kathie was packed in the sleigh by mamma's side, but not a word was spoken during the short drive. There was no time to spare. Dr. Markham went for the ticket, and directly afterward the engine gave its warning sound. Just a moment for a parting kiss, and she was hurried in, but Kathie caught a glimpse of her at the window. Then the train moved away slowly.

"Come, little Dame Durden," exclaimed the doctor, finding her warm hand.

Kathie was trying very hard not to sob outright, but take a little cry softly. She had hardly thought that she would feel quite so broken-hearted.

"My little girl," said the doctor, as he put his

shaggy coat-sleeve around her, "it is a sore trial, and you would have less than a child's heart if you did not feel its bitterness. You have been very brave so far. We will take a little drive around and get some good spirits to carry back to auntie."

Jenny, who was as black as a coal and had been pretty mettlesome in her young days, pricked up her ears at her master's voice, and after they turned into a quiet street flew along as if she was enjoying a good race. Kathie wiped away the tears and summoned all her courage, trying to think of the happy time two months distant. It seemed very long, looking ahead, but then she had already been in the city more than that length of time, so it would pass after a while.

The remainder of the day was pretty quiet both for herself and Aunt Ruth. Neither felt disposed to talk much, and perhaps it was as well. Now and then a great pang of homesickness and longing came over her, and at night she quietly cried herself to sleep; not that she wished to return and leave Aunt Ruth alone, but her tender little heart yearned for the others.

Mrs. Havens sent for her to come to tea one evening, and entertained her very charmingly with some collections of pictures she had just received. There was a beautiful series of marine plants, sea-ferns, and many curiosities, and Mrs. Havens related some interesting facts about them.

Ada sent her an invitation for Saturday. Some friends of Mrs. Meredith, from Cuba, were staying with them, and as there were two girls they would like Kathie to join them. " Be in the best possible voice," wrote Ada.

But on Friday the arrangements were changed. A new engagement had been made for Saturday, and Ada begged her to come on Sunday, as their friends expected to leave for Washington on the day following. Mr. Edward Meredith brought the message. "They all feel very sorry, and will be a good deal disappointed if you don't come. Then I should really like to have you see these young Cubans, for they are extremely odd and piquant. It will only be a quiet little supper."

Kathie ran up to consult Aunt Ruth.

" I don't quite approve of Sunday visiting ; but this is under peculiar circumstances ; do just as you like about it."

15

So Kathie concluded to go, since Mr. Meredith was very much in earnest.

"I'll come for you," he said with his good-by. "Quite early too, I think, so be ready by a little after three."

Kathie went to church in the morning with Mrs. Markham. She was beginning to feel quite happy and reconciled again. After dinner she read to Aunt Ruth awhile, and then dressed herself in her pretty blue merino, and brushed her long curls until they shone.

"Don't forget what day it is, Kathie," Aunt Ruth said as she kissed her, for the servant announced that the carriage was at the door.

Instead of Mr. Meredith only, there was a whole carriage full, and Kathie started in a little surprise.

"We were all going to vespers," explained Uncle Edward, "so we thought we would call for you first." And then he introduced her to Madame Hernadez, and the two girls, Julie and Romena.

Madame Hernadez was very brilliant and stylish-looking, with the blackest of eyes and hair. The girls were not nearly so pretty. Julie, fourteen, but

very small of her age, was rather thin and sallow.
Romena had a lovely color in her cheeks, and her
eyes were much brighter.

Uncle Edward took Kathie on the seat with him,
but she felt very odd and strange. Ada was talking
French with Julie, and feeling rather proud of her
acquirements.

"You have never been to a vesper service, — have
you ? " Mr. Meredith asked of Kathie.

"No," she answered, in a low tone.

"The music is really magnificent at St. Francis.
I often drop in to hear it."

"You have some beautiful churches here," exclaimed Madame, "but they all look so new. No
old ruins nor ancient shrines."

"And we are a new people," he answered, with a
peculiar smile.

They soon reached the church, which was not
crowded, though service was just commencing. An
usher very politely seated them. Kathie felt somewhat awkward and uncomfortable, but Ada adapted
herself to the situation with admirable grace. The
others were very devout.

There was a series of prayers in Latin, with musi-

cal interruptions, and then the place was filled with
clouds of incense.   After that the music became
more of a chant, and the organ was most exquisitely
played.   The church seemed to grow darker, and the
weird waves of melody affected Kathie. strangely.
Some sad, soft swells that almost brought the tears
to her eyes, and then the voices of the singers
rising in pathetic strains.   It was all unintelligible
to her, to be sure, but she had too much reverence to
be inattentive in any place of worship.

Ada was quite eloquent in her appreciation of
the music, and she discussed the service with the
air of a devotee.   Kathie and Romena made a little
acquaintance, but it was not until they were at home
and had taken off their hats and cloaks that they
began to feel at all familiar.

Sunday was always considered as a sort of holiday at the Merediths'.   Uncle Edward rejoined the
gentlemen in the smoking-room, Madame and Mrs.
Meredith fell into a trifling conversation, and Ada
began to tell Kathie about their going to the theatre
on Saturday evening and an opera *matinée* in the
morning.   Between, there had been quite an elegant
hotel dinner given to the Hernadez by some Cuban
friends.

"Two of the gentlemen are coming here to-night," she whispered, "and I think them so handsome."

Then Kathie must come up stairs and see what elegant ball-dresses the girls had. Julie grew quite animated on this subject, and made her displays with no little pride. It sounded very pretty to hear her talk in broken English, now and then using a Spanish phrase or sentence when at a loss to express herself.

In the midst of this entertainment the supper-bell rang. Another lady and gentleman had arrived, and somehow Kathie could not help wishing herself at home. This feast that seemed almost like a party was so different from her quiet Sunday-night talks with Aunt Ruth.

The four girls had their end of the table, and Ada played hostess with a great deal of grace. There was a profusion of creams and jellies, and two pyramids of handsome hot-house flowers. The new-comer, Mrs. Henriques, was every elegantly dressed in a light silk, cut low in the neck and trimmed with white lace.

They sat a long while at the table, until Kathie began to grow really tired. As they were return-

ing to the drawing-room Mrs. Henriques paused
until she came up in range.

"What lovely hair this young lady has!" she exclaimed, twining it around her fingers. "I was not
sure that it was all real."

"Real!" echoed Kathie, in surprise, and then she
blushed, half frightened at having spoken.

"Your own, I meant, but you are hardly old
enough for such things. When you go into society
you will find these long golden curls worth a fortune
to you. Look, Mr. Hernadez, did you ever see a more
exquisite color?"

"But the child is such a perfect blonde! You will
make many a heart ache in the course of a few
years"; and he bowed gallantly.

Kathie blushed deeper than ever and tried to
shrink away. Madame Hernadez closed her in on
the other side, however, and began to compliment her.

"But you are quite too shy, *ma belle,*" she said, in a
most winning tone.

At this juncture the two gentlemen were announced,— Cubans also, and brothers ; but the younger,
who was less than twenty, was exceedingly handsome.
Ada went forward to meet him with the air of a

grown-up lady. He exchanged a few words with Julie Hernadez, and then devoted himself to Ada, the attention appearing to elate her greatly.

"We were to have some music," began Madame Hernadez. "One of these young gentlemen is an excellent pianist."

And so Ada's charming *tête-à-tête* was broken up; but she and Julie, who was evidently a coquette, young as she appeared, stationed themselves within range.

After playing several pieces he paused and spoke to Mrs. Meredith, who summoned her daughter with a glance.

"Mr. De Castro wishes you and Kathie to sing. Kathie!" elevating her voice a little.

Kathie rose from her seat between the two ladies and came shyly forward. Mr. De Castro remarked for the first time how very pretty she was.

Mrs. Meredith gave her a special introduction.

"We want you and Ada to sing," she said. She was very proud of her daughter's fine voice, but being alto it was not so rich or perfect in soprano parts.

"O Mrs. Meredith!" and Kathie's heart was in her throat. "I do not believe I can. I —"

"Nonsense!" was the rather sharp reply. "Why, you have practised so much together! Don't be foolish!"

Every pulse was in a quiver. Kathie wondered if she could acquit herself even tolerably. Then Mrs. Henriques came forward and gave her a bright smile.

"What do you know?" asked Mr. De Castro, glancing at her encouragingly.

"O, Ada, that Evening Hymn to the Virgin!" exclaimed Julie. "You know you promised me, and it is mamma's favorite."

Mr. De Castro found it, and ran his fingers lightly through the accompaniment.

Kathie was wondering in her heart if it was strictly a "Sunday tune." She was a good deal frightened and confused, and when he said "Ready," she obeyed from her usual habit. Her voice trembled visibly, but as Ada's swelled clear and strong, she took courage.

They did sing very beautifully together. The ladies made a circle around them, and even the gentlemen were attracted. When they came to the refrain, "Ora pro nobis," the melody was absolutely touching.

" O, how lovely ! how charming ! " and Mrs. Henriques stooped to kiss them both.

" This is indeed a treat," exclaimed Mr. Hernadez. " Why, I did not know that you had so much amateur musical talent. De Castro, we shall keep you busy the remainder of the evening. Young ladies, you must be indulgent."

" You were humming something yesterday that I liked so much, Miss Ada. You said you sang it with a friend "; and Madame Hernadez gave her an eager glance.

Ada bowed her head gracefully, affecting to think.

" Was it Natalie, the mill song ? "

" It had a very beautiful chorus, — tra la, — a sort of wild, ringing melody."

" O, I remember, — the Gypsy's Chorus."

" They sing that finely, I think," said Mrs. Meredith.

Mr. De Castro, guided by Ada, soon found it. But there had been a great struggle going on within Kathie's heart and conscience. This was a gay little opera song with an echo that was peculiarly adapted to Ada's voice. The simplest and easiest way would be to sing it. They would never think any the less of her, and to refuse would make such a scene.

Just at this moment her talk with General Mackenzie recurred to her. He had said that they were all soldiers, and though their great Captain might not reprimand or punish, his eye was never off them. She felt that all at home would disapprove of her singing such a song on the hallowed Sunday evening.

The accompaniment sounded dreamily in her ears as she glanced around. All the faces were expectant, and she understood quite indifferent to the effort she must make alone. Mamma trusted her to do nothing that she could not conscientiously approve, but the trial was dreadful, and she trembled as if in an ague.

"Ada," she said, with a gasp, "I cannot sing it."

"Why, yes, you can," returned Ada, in surprise.

"No — I mean that — "

Mr. De Castro struck the note.

"There," said Ada, "begin!"

Kathie made a movement away and turned very pale. "If you will excuse me," she said to some one, and that happened to be Mrs. Meredith.

"Why, what is the matter, child?"

"I think it — not quite right — for Sunday!"

It seemed to her that she had said the most dreadful, disobliging, and impertinent thing she could utter.

"Can't she, mamma?" began Ada, disappointedly.

Mrs. Meredith bridled in a dignified and rather austere fashion. "I suppose I am the best judge of what is to be done in my own house," she exclaimed, with cutting emphasis; "and a simple little song like that can harm no one."

"I would rather not," Kathie said, in her sweetest manner, though she could not keep the tears from her eyes.

"What is the trouble?" asked Mr. De Castro, turning his soft dark eyes upon Kathie.

Mrs. Henriques besieged her on the other side, and it seemed to her that she had better yield.

"Uncle Edward," said Ada, "I wish you would come and talk to Kathie. She has taken an obstinate freak in her head and will not sing." Then she added in a whisper, meant only for Kathie's ears, "It's real mean! I believe you do it because you 're jealous and don't want me to be admired!"

All this seemed to happen in a moment. Uncle Edward leaned over and caught sight of the tearful eyes.

"What is it, Kathie?"

The kind voice almost unnerved her, but she would make one more effort.

"I would rather not sing this song on Sunday night," she said, in a low tone. "I don't mean to be cross or disobliging —" and she paused, for she could not utter another word.

Mr. Meredith laughed. "If no one ever did anything worse than singing such a song on Sunday —"

"O, is that the trouble?" said Mrs. Henriques. "Why, what a little puritan!"

"The child is quite right if she does not feel like it," exclaimed Mr. De Castro, who had been studying the expression of her face. "I always respect the religious scruples of another."

Kathie gave him a most grateful look.

"Perhaps there is something else you can sing."

"We will excuse Miss Kathie," rejoined Mrs. Meredith, haughtily, and she turned away.

The party around the piano broke up and scattered to different portions of the room.

"What an odd child!" said Mrs. Henriques, passing her arm around Kathie. "Do you think we are all so very careless and wicked?"

" I don't want to think anything about others," she replied, barely repressing a sob. " Mamma would not like to hear me sing the song, and I felt that I ought to do just what I would if she were here."

" She is very brave and true," added Mr. De Castro, and somehow the look encouraged her.

CHAPTER XIV.

OUT OF THE SHADOW AND IN THE SUN.

But the charm of the evening was gone for Kathie. Mrs. Meredith was too well bred to allow any awkwardness to fall upon her guests, and covered the little scene with a gay conversation. Mr. Meredith wanted very much to cross over to Kathie and comfort her, but he was in the midst of a discussion with Mr. Hernadez. She sat beside Mrs. Henriques, looking quite forlorn, and wishing that she could go home. Then Mr. De Castro began to talk to her, much to Ada's vexation. He was very pleasant, and though he did not share her scruples, for his education had been so very different, he honored her courage in avowing them.

"Is your mamma in the city?" he asked.

"No," returned Kathie. And then she explained that she was staying with an aunt who was here for medical treatment.

"You are very fond of music," he continued, with a smile. "Are you studying?"

"A little," she answered, timidly.

"And your voice is exceedingly sweet and smooth. You ought to have an excellent teacher. I should like to hear you in some other pieces. I suppose you sing a good deal."

"When I am at home," returned Kathie.

Ada could no longer endure the sight of Mr. De Castro's attention to another. She called him to explain to them the name of some tropical flower, and then she and Julie exerted their charms to the utmost. She might venture to deal more generously with Julie, as that young lady was so soon to leave the city.

Mrs. Henriques changed her seat, and Kathie was left alone. Every one in the room seemed happy and engrossed except herself. And then the little French clock on the mantel struck the half-hour. At nine she must go home.

The moments were long and wearisome. She counted the seconds and prayed for them to go faster. She did not dare to leave her seat, for a feeling of awkwardness chained her to it. Mr. Meredith, glancing up suddenly, took in the position of the drooping and dispirited face, and brought his argument to a rather abrupt close.

"My dear child," he said, approaching her, "you should not let such a trifling mischance cloud your evening. After all, it was of very little account."

"I should like to go home," she made answer, in a tremulous voice. "Aunt Ruth told me to come at nine."

"Which gives you fifteen minutes' grace. Shall we go over and talk to Ada and Julie?"

"I would rather go home"; and this time her voice was full of tears.

"My child, you shall do as you like. It is a fine night, so suppose I walk with you, instead of sending you in the carriage?"

Kathie gave him a bright, grateful look.

"Very well. Make your adieus then."

That was a great trial. She had half a mind to slip unnoticed out of the room, but Mr. Meredith smoothed the way for her by announcing her departure to the girls and to Mrs. Henriques, who was in their vicinity.

"What makes you go so soon?" asked Ada, languidly.

Mrs. Henriques kissed her warmly, and this broke the spell of reserve.

"I am sorry about the singing," said Madame Hernadez, in a low tone. "If we were not going to-morrow, I should ask to have the visit repeated."

That comforted Kathie a good deal, the tone in which it was spoken being so frank and pleasant.

Kathie thought she ought to make some apology to Mrs. Meredith, but although that lady dismissed her very graciously, there was an air about her that showed the child she still felt offended.

"Will you order the carriage, Edward?" she asked of her brother-in-law.

He nodded and left the room. Ada, as a matter of courtesy, followed her friend.

"It was a shame for you to spoil the evening, Kathie," she began.

"Hush," said Uncle Edward. "It was right for Kathie to honor her mother as well in her absence as in her presence."

Kathie hurried on her wrappings and uttered her good-by, but Ada was not very cordial, it must be confessed.

It was so good to get out in the fresh air that Kathie drew a long breath of rapture. The moon

16

was shining at its brightest, albeit it was a midwinter moon, and the atmosphere keen and frosty.

"My dear little friend," Mr. Meredith began, presently, "I regret so much that your visit has been spoiled. If you thought singing the song wrong, no one should have urged you."

"I am afraid Mrs. Meredith considered me rude and — foolish about it. I did not mean that I thought myself better than the others — "

"My dear Kathie, we could not suspect you of that. As for Mrs. Meredith, on sober consideration she will see that your course was right, even if the virtue was a little overstrained."

Kathie's heart beat rapidly. Must she lose his good opinion also?

"Why did you think it so very wrong?" and Mr. Meredith gave a light little laugh, which showed that he treated it as a matter of small importance.

Kathie was a good deal troubled. What could she say to make him understand her feelings? And as she was casting about in perplexity, the best of all reasons came into her mind.

"Remember the Sabbath day to keep it holy." Her voice was low but earnest, and something in it touched Mr. Meredith.

" Mamma, and Aunt Ruth, and Uncle Robert would have felt very sorry to hear of my singing such a song on Sunday evening.   I don't know as the other was quite right.   I did not have hardly time to think of it."

" You were right in not doing a thing of which you felt certain they would disapprove."

" And because there was a higher right.   I need not have told them, you know, and they would never ask me.   I am glad now that I did n't, only it almost broke my heart to displease everybody."

She uttered this so simply that he could see there had been no spirit of ostentation in her soul.

" All those people have been brought up so differently," he said, " and are used to going to concerts and all kinds of amusements on Sunday evenings.   I suppose Mrs. Meredith thought only of their entertainment, and Ada's voice sounds so beautifully with yours."

Kathie imagined there was something a little regretful in his tone.

" Are you sorry ? " she asked, humbly.

" Not that you had the courage to do right in so simple yet perplexing a matter.   And now you must forgive and forget."

Kathie felt that this would be an easy matter for her if she was not reminded of it too often.

"And here we are at Dr. Markham's. How short the walk has been!"

He looked smilingly into Kathie's face, which was grave and sweet, and so full of childhood's innocence that he was deeply moved.

"God bless you," he said, in an earnest tone, "and keep you as pure and steadfast in the truth as you are now. Heaven knows the world has need enough of good women!"

Kathie just paused in the library to speak to Mrs. Markham, and then walked slowly up stairs.

"Did you have a nice time?" asked Aunt Ruth.

"The girls were very odd and foreign," she answered, "but the ladies and gentlemen were pleasant."

Dr. Markham had forbidden conversations of any length at bedtime, and Kathie still adhered scrupulously to the command, though she longed to open her sore little heart to Aunt Ruth, who could understand her so well. Mr. Meredith's manner had pained her somewhat, and she wondered if any one ever appreciated the great effort a person must make continually to be good. Even tender and generous

Charlie Darrell had once called her queer when she had just made a sacrifice of her own pleasure. And it seemed now that she wanted mamma more than ever, for she felt utterly friendless and forlorn.

So it was a great relief to confess on the next day, and receive a little comfort. Kathie was not at all given to exaggeration, but told a story in a simple, straightforward manner.

"I am afraid Mrs. Meredith thought me impertinent and obtrusive, but I did not mean to be," Kathie said, deprecatingly. "I am very sorry that I went, for we looked over the ball-dresses and pretty things, and talked about them until it seemed quite like a week-day."

"And this is why I disapprove of Sunday visiting in most cases, though it would have appeared rather discourteous to refuse. I do not see how you could well have done differently, and I am thankful that you had the courage to confess the truth. It is hard to suffer ill consequences when one has taken the only right course, but you must bear it patiently."

"I don't suppose they will ever ask me again. I believe I don't love Ada very much, Aunt Ruth, for she so often makes me uncomfortable; but they have all been very kind to me."

"So they have, my dear, and I regret a rupture. There are a good many trials in this life, Kathie, and so far your stay here has scarcely been shadowed from any outside cause. You must try to be just as happy as usual, let the result be what it may."

She might have been a trifle more grave, perhaps, but no one save Aunt Ruth knew of her secret trouble. The matter was not to end there, however. Some days afterward Mrs. Havens called, and hough she was always fond of Kathie, her greeting now was quite extravagant.

"My dear little girl," she exclaimed, "I heard an incident about you that filled my heart with joy,—the occurrence at Mrs. Meredith's last Sunday evening. I am glad to know that you are not ashamed to bear witness for the truth."

Kathie colored painfully.

"We had talked the subject over and dismissed it," explained Aunt Ruth. "It was rather an unfortunate affair."

"Nay, I do not think so. Of course the Cuban party were accustomed to such entertainments, but Mrs. Meredith said that although she was vexed at the moment, and much disappointed at having her guests miss the song, she honored Kathie for not being persuaded to do what she did not consider right.

"Did she say that?" exclaimed Kathie, in amaze, her sweet face flushing with delight.

"Yes, my dear, and much more. Don't allow it to make you vain, for there is no charm like perfect simplicity."

"I am so glad that she is not angry. But I wonder — if Mr. Edward Meredith — "

"You will not lose in his estimation by such an act, I assure you."

It seemed to Kathie then that she was perfectly happy. And when, on the following Sunday morning, she received a basket of lovely hot-house flowers with a card attached, on which was written, "with the kind regards of Mrs. Emily Meredith," Kathie felt that it was a peace-offering, and if one hard thought had lingered she would have banished it then. Uncle Edward made a flying trip to Cedarwood, and when he returned, with loads of love and the best of news, he was doubly welcome to Kathie.

February came in quite mild. The snow nearly all melted away, and for several days there was a bright, warm sun. Aunt Ruth improved rapidly. She was

allowed to walk around a little, though still compelled
to use her crutch, as Dr. Markham thought it hardly
safe to bear so much weight on her yet enfeebled
limb. One of these bright days he proposed to take
her out in an easy carriage.

Kathie was delighted. That really looked like
getting well. And though Aunt Ruth was bundled
up and carried down stairs, she came back with a
faint tinge of pink in her cheeks, and the brightest
light in her eye that had been there for a long time.

Kathie wrote home a most glowing letter. It had
the effect of bringing Uncle Robert at once, though
he declared that his principal errand was to see if
Kathie was in possession of her senses.

"To think that we can go home in a month if
Aunt Ruth does n't have any relapse!" she said,
dancing round. "Dear old Cedarwood, and Rob,
and Fred, and everybody!"

"And that 's all my reward?" growled the doctor.
"If you were real generous you would propose to
stay a month at least with me!"

Kathie's bright face grew suddenly grave. "I
don't know how I could stay away from mamma,"
she said, pleadingly.

"Would n't Mrs. Markham make a good mamma, I want to know?"

"But she would not be quite your own, — would she, Kathie?" exclaimed Mrs. Markham, with a sweet smile.

Kathie nestled lovingly at her side. She had made many dear friends during this stay, — friends who would not soon forget the cheerful and sweet-tempered little girl.

In one respect the time appeared to go rapidly with Kathie, and in another slowly. The days were busy and happy. There were little keepsakes to make for one and another, visiting, music, and rides with Aunt Ruth, who now went out on every fine day. Uncle Robert took her while he stayed, and then Mr. Meredith begged that he might be allowed to make himself useful whenever the doctor was busy. He and Kathie had taken up their old friendship without a word; indeed, she had been reinstated in her former place, but Ada seemed rather disposed to be captious. It appeared to her that Kathie created quite too much interest for an unstylish little body, who was never elegantly dressed, and who had no particular accomplishments.

It was the looking forward that was so interminable to Kathie. When she said " Three weeks to wait," on Monday morning, it was like apportioning a lifetime.

" Kathie," exclaimed Aunt Ruth, laughingly, one day, " I believe I would restrict my vision. If the time appears so long, I would n't look at the end."

" But I think about going home continually."

" Suppose you say, then, ' We will go home as soon as Aunt Ruth gets well ' ? "

" That would seem such an indefinite limit. And I don't really make myself unhappy."

" Nor impatient ? "

" Well, only a little, sometimes. I don't see how you can be so patient," she exclaimed, suddenly.

" My dear child, after waiting years, a few weeks appear a very short space of time. Indeed, I sometimes think that it must be a happy dream. To go back to our lovely home sound and well in body, and able to help myself, is like a leaf out of your fairyland."

" Yes, I used to wish to be a fairy, — did n't I ? " and Kathie's eyes wandered dreamily to the floating clouds in the sky. " It has all come about just as I desired. I could not have done any better if I had possessed a magic wand."

" 'All things shall work together for good if they love Him,' " repeated Aunt Ruth, reverently.

There was a great rejoicing when she began to walk about without any cane, and when she could go down stairs Kathie was wild with delight.

"You may write home as soon as you like," Dr. Markham said to Kathie, " and the first fair day we will pronounce you discharged. I think your mother had better come, though."

Kathie kissed the doctor in her transport, and he wanted to know if she had resolved to remain with him, which brought her to her senses immediately.

No one rejoiced more truly in their good fortune than Mrs. Havens. She had been won by the patience and sweetness displayed so unaffectedly during Miss Conover's long and trying illness, and the childlike graces of Kathie.

"We shall all miss you very much," she said. " I am so glad that I happened to meet you last summer, and I shall always be proud to number your mother and your aunt among my choicest friends, while you may always be sure of a warm corner in my heart."

The music lessons were given up, though Mrs. Gifford was very sorry to part with her promising pupil.

"Now you must ask your uncle for a piano," she said. "With the necessary application you will make a fine performer."

Kathie thought that this would be her first petition after they were settled at home.

Mamma and Uncle Robert made their appearance speedily. Then it had to rain, and afterward blow off cold as midwinter.

"The fates are against you," said the doctor to Kathie. "You will have to stay until April."

So long as mamma was there the disappointment was not very keen. Mrs. Alston kept pretty busy packing, receiving a few calls, and doing a little shopping.

And then dawned a lovely spring-like day. Nearly all her friends had been in to say good by to Kathie, and she was quite ready to start at a moment's notice. The trunks were sent down in the hall, and after breakfast the doctor had a long talk with his patient. She might be a trifle lame always, but it would never inconvenience her seriously, and her general health she would doubtless find much improved. He had taken a great interest in her from the first, and was glad that he had been able to do so much for her.

Miss Conover was more than thankful. For the kindly care and gentle words of encouragement in her apparently hopeless hours she could make no return save the most sincere gratitude. The tears that filled her eyes and the tremulous curve of her lips attested this.

The doctor pretended to think it very unkind that Kathie should desire to leave them, but they finally compromised matters by promising each other a visit.

" 'The last and fatal hour has come,' " said Uncle Robert, gayly. " The carriage is at the door, and we have not much time to lose."

They said their farewells with tears, for it had been a pleasant home to them at Dr. Markham's. Uncle Robert handed them all in, and the door was shut; but Kathie smiled sadly out of the window to the two standing in the hall.

A very comfortable journey without any incident, but when they reached Brookside station everything looked very queer to Kathie's city eyes. The houses were small, the streets unpaved, and even the church steeple did not seem as high as formerly.

" But there 's Rob and the ponies, so I guess' it is all right," she exclaimed, laughingly; "dear little fellows, how I shall enjoy them again!"

Uncle Robert assisted them out on the platform, and Rob made a rush at everybody, not minding in the least if he did kiss them in the street. Kathie had to stop and look at him, — he had grown so large!

" It 's splendid to see you walking along like other folks," he said to Aunt Ruth. " I feel as if I wanted to give the loudest kind of whoop and hurrah! Why, I can hardly believe it!"

"I can hardly believe it here myself," she answered, smilingly; "I have always gone limping around at Brookside."

A few neighbors who happened to be within sight thronged around and congratulated them. Then they drove on to Cedarwood.

There it was, sure enough. Clumps and walks of evergreens, and the rippling lake, making a silvery background. The Morrisons all at the gate, and

little Jamie waving his cap in great glee.   Four
months since Kathie had seen it, and her luminous
eyes filled with tears.   Home would always be the
dearest place to her.

There was Freddy on the wide porch with a great
green and scarlet parrot, who nodded his head, and
screeched out of his hooked bill, " Welcome, Kathie !
welcome, Aunt Ruth !"

" And I taught him all myself," exclaimed Fred,
eagerly, the words almost drowned in kisses ; "he
can ask for anything, Kathie."

" But look at Aunt Ruth !" said Rob.

" O, where 's her crutch ?   Can she walk all
alone ?" and Fred stared in wide-eyed wonder.

" All alone, my boy," replied the soft voice.

" Well, miss, if I ever expected to see the day !"
was Hannah's ejaculation, as she held up both hands;
" and, Miss Kathie, darling, we 've had a lonely
time without you.   It 's hardly been like the same
house."

" I 'm so glad to get back, — so glad and thankful
for everything !"

Aunt Ruth lay down on the sofa at once, and
Kathie took away her numerous wrappings.   Rob

seated himself beside her, and told her, with boyish bashfulness, that she was as pretty as any young girl.

Kathie had to make a tour of the house, even to the top of the tower. There was Aunt Ruth's room full of tender spring twilight, softened by the crimson tints; and here her own, a perfect marvel of prettiness and comfort. She did not envy Ada her more costly appointments.

Supper was quite late. How delightful it was to see them all around the table again, so bright and happy! Freddy had so much to tell that he was hardly half through when the rest were done; but mamma was indulgent on this night. She even allowed him to sit up until long past his bedtime.

Finally, in their talking, they came to the Christmas-tree; and Kathie said it had been so nice to have them remember her in her absence.

"O," exclaimed Fred, "they did n't send you all! there 's a great big —"

"Hush, Fred! Uncle Robert, let us take Kathie to see it, though it did not come off of the Christmas-tree exactly."

She sprang up, and, escorted by the two, entered the parlor.   At first she saw nothing unusual; but as they neared one end she uttered an exclamation of surprise and joy.   There was her piano!   "Oh!" she said, "how did you keep the secret!   Dear Uncle Robert!" and the rest was lost in happy tears, as she clasped her arms around his neck.

When the house was all silent, and everybody going to bed, Kathie crept into mamma's room to say a last good-night to Aunt Ruth, and found her kneeling reverently.   In a moment she was beside her, slipping her own hand in the one so soft and warm.   "Dear Aunt Ruth," she whispered, in a voice that was full of deepest joy, "I do not believe there are two people in all the world to whom God has been as good.   We ought to praise him, and be thankful for the rest of our lives"; and the prayer ended with a tender kiss.

THE END.

University Press: John Wilson & Son, Cambridge.

MISS DOUGLAS'S BOOKS.

UNIFORM BINDING. PRICE $1.50 EACH.

Whom Kathie Married.
The Old Woman who lived in a Shoe.
Lost in a Great City.
Hope Mills; or, between Friend and Sweet-
    heart.
Home Nook; or, the Crown of Duty.
In Trust; or, Dr. Bertram's Household.
Nelly Kinnard's Kingdom.
From Hand to Mouth.
Stephen Dare.
Claudia.
Sydnie Adriance; or, Trying his Hand.
Seven Daughters.

KATHIE STORIES FOR YOUNG PEOPLE.

SIX VOLUMES. ILLUSTRATED. PER VOLUME, $1.00.

In the Ranks.
Kathie's Three Wishes.
Kathie's Aunt Ruth.
Kathie's Summer at Cedarwood.
Kathie's Soldiers.
Kathie's Harvest-Days.

Santa Claus Land.   (*In press.*)

Sold by all booksellers, and sent by mail, post-
paid, on receipt of price.

LEE AND SHEPARD, Publishers.

www.ingramcontent.com/pod-product-compliance
Lightning Source LLC
Chambersburg PA
CBHW020354030726
47496CB00007B/2132